BROKEN
SHARDS
of TIME

BROKEN SHARDS of TIME

NYAH NICHOL

COMMON DEER PRESS

Published in 2020 by Common Deer Press
3203-1 Scott St.
Toronto, ON
M5E 1A1

This book is a work of fiction. Names, characters, places, and incidents are
either the product of the author's imagination or are used fictitiously.

Library of Congress Cataloging-in-Publication Data
Nyah Nichol—First edition.
Broken Shards of Time / Nyah Nichols
ISBN 978-1-988761-48-0 (print)
ISBN 978-1-988761-49-7 (e-book)

Cover and interior designer, David Moratto

Printed in Canada

www.commondeerpress.com

This book is dedicated to

Mom and Dad, the most amazing parents ever;
Silas, my brother and bestie;
Everett, my sister and proud owner of two hermit crabs,
Hermie and Hermie 2.0;
Grace, my godmother, who is a writer like me;
and Titus, my crazy little brother, who sometimes
wears two pairs of underwear.

PART ONE
WREN DERECHO

⇛ 2 HOURS and 59 MINUTES to SILEO TERRA

May 27, 2070, 9:01 pm...

I didn't think it would come to this.

I never intended to be against the world.

Now I was about to face my greatest enemy: myself.

One of us had to win.

One of us had to fight harder.

One of us had to be stronger.

I chose what was right, yet somehow it was wrong.

I tried to write my own destiny, but my story was engraved in stone.

The past had moulded me, but I refused to let it define me.

I followed the path I had carved out, yet I was unfamiliar with where I ended up.

I selected the best option but wound up with the worst outcome.

The future seemed like an endless maze, yet too suddenly, it passed.

That was how I ended up here.

I had gotten myself into this crazy upside-down catastrophe, and now I had to find my way out of it.

18 YEARS, 2 MONTHS, 11 DAYS, 9 HOURS, and 15 MINUTES to SILEO TERRA

March 16, 2052, 1:04 pm...

"Stormy, can you get in the car?" Mom asked impatiently as she popped her head into my room. Her cropped hair, styled in a pixie cut, was a darker auburn than mine. I studied the freckles sprinkled across her face. I liked how they softened her stern expression. She spun around and disappeared down the hall.

"Yeah, yeah," I muttered. My name wasn't Stormy, but my parents liked to call me that because when I got angry, I resembled a storm. My real name was Wren Derecho.

Annoyed, I reluctantly put the book down on my nightstand. I always read to calm my mind. After an argument I'd had with my mom earlier that day, it had felt soothing to dive into another world. My mom's disruption yanked me unwillingly from the story I was engulfed in. I'd been irritated because Dad had said he was leaving again for "an extended period of time" after we visited my uncle. He always left with barely a day's warning, and my mom just went along with it, cancelling appointments and postponing plans with friends and family. It made my blood boil. I'd told my mom it wasn't fair that our schedules always had to revolve around Dad and his work, but deep down, I was just upset he wouldn't be around again.

Still sulking a little, I trudged down the winding staircase and through the short hallway to the garage door. My uncle, William Derecho, wanted to show my father something he had been working

4

on. Naturally, I, too, was curious. Uncle William was a skilled and talented inventor, a scientist of sorts who worked for a government organization called the Department of Advanced Innovation and Research, but my father and his associates just referred to it as DAIR. My uncle was everything I wanted to be when I grew up. I loved spending time with him, working on our special experiments. The last time I saw him, he let me help him build a fully functional miniature-sized rocket outside the government facility. He even let me attach the nose cone all by myself.

I slammed our sedan's door shut and waited in the backseat, staring out the window and absentmindedly twisting a piece of my red hair around my finger. My dad's voice startled me, and I turned to see him staring at his phone in the shadows of the garage. As my eyes adjusted to the darkness, his familiar square frame leaning against the workbench became more visible. I noticed the salt and pepper patches that had just recently started appearing on the sides of his clean-cut brown hair made him look more sophisticated.

"Looks like they're starting early," he mumbled, pulling at his bottom lip with his thumb and index finger. He always did that when he was nervous. My dad worked for the same obscure organization as my uncle. However, he spent most of his days travelling instead of working at the large government headquarters, even though a lot of the projects he helped with were stored there. He was secretive about his work and rarely said a word about it to anyone. All I knew was that he specialized in sourcing out uncommon materials. Dad had once told me there were secrets stored within the drab walls and cracked bricks of the large building—secrets containing ancient and modern-day breakthroughs. Uncle William said that one day, those secrets would ultimately save the world.

Dad slid into the passenger seat. "Stormy, you need to remember to be careful and to stay out of the way. The work they're doing is dangerous..." I stopped listening as he rambled on about all the rules I had to follow. Sometimes I thought Dad forgot I was ten years old now.

It was going to be a long car ride but so worth it. I couldn't wait to see Uncle William because I knew he would set up a fun experiment to do with me.

As soon as Mom jumped into the driver's seat, we hit the road. I drummed my fingers on the armrest and gazed out the window. After more than an hour of riding in silence, I noticed dark clouds beginning to gather above us while Dad made yet another phone call. He was pretty much on his phone for work all the time. That's why Mom usually drove.

"Is it just me, or is it getting darker out?" I asked. My eyes scanned and searched the sky. Suddenly, a great crash of thunder shook the whole car, shattering our peaceful drive. The thunder was followed quickly by a blinding flash of lightning. My mom slammed on the brakes, and my heart began pounding so hard, I thought it would burst out of my chest.

Blurred lights flashed continuously, just like the searing pain coursing through my body. My parents had been here a second ago. It didn't make any sense. I didn't know what to do. I didn't know what to feel. I didn't know what to think.

The skeleton of the sedan still surrounded me, and I was aware of my seatbelt holding me in tightly. Lightning and thunder encircled me, drawing my attention to the storm outside.

"HELP ME, PLEASE!" I tried to force out the words gurgling in the back of my throat but failed miserably. With every agonizing second that passed, I felt myself fading away.

Seconds felt like hours. So much pain. And then darkness.

Time passed. I drifted in and out of consciousness, but I was dimly aware I wasn't trapped in the car anymore. The next thing I knew, I heard voices that seemed distant, yet somehow, I knew they were not. My ears struggled to work properly.

"She will die."

A few faint words in the ever-spreading darkness squirmed their way into my mind. I felt a thin sheet that had been loosely laid over my body being pulled up to my chin.

"We haven't tested it on humans yet."

The voices were so familiar, yet I could not recognize them.

"It's the only thing that can save her."

18 YEARS, 2 MONTHS, 8 DAYS, 23 HOURS, and 53 MINUTES to SILEO TERRA

March 19, 2052, 12:07 am...

A ching all over, I rolled onto my side. My body felt stiff, and my eyes flickered open to see I was in a room with dazzling lights and walls that felt like they were about to close in on me. My eyes hurt from the bright lights, so I closed them again. I struggled to lift my hand to brush away the matted auburn tresses from my face, but it was just too hard, so I gave up.

As I tried opening my eyes again, something flashed, reflecting the artificial light, but I couldn't recognize it. Icy pain covered my forehead. Something was wrong. I opened and closed my mouth, trying to produce moisture for my tongue and throat. My heart started to race. Finally, I managed to raise my arm, and I heard a soft clink when my fingers reached my cheek. A slow, dreadful chill crept throughout my body. Panic filled me as I realized the flash of light had come from my hand. Both my hands felt so heavy. I painfully leaned over the side of the bed and saw a distorted reflection of my face in the shiny tile floor. A hoarse cry escaped from my mouth as I stared at the smooth, hard substance spread across one side of my face. It was the same material as the metal around my fingers. Metal. METAL?!

Uncle William entered the room then and ran over to me. "Wren, it's okay. You're okay. You're safe. I'm here."

He leaned over and pulled me close. I slowly wrapped my arms around him, thankful to see someone familiar. Tears collected in my eyes as I looked up at him. He gently helped me lie back down on the bed and perched on the edge of the bed close to me.

I croaked, "Where am I? How long have I been here? Where a-are Mom and Dad?" My voice trembled; I was terrified of the answers about to tumble out of his mouth.

Uncle William didn't cry very often, so I was shocked to see his eyes so red and puffy, with dark pits circling his deep eye sockets. Uncle William bowed his head low, avoiding my urgent, pleading eyes, and pushed back his straw-like blonde hair.

"We couldn't...they were...they didn't make it." He gulped, choking back tears.

No, he must have been mistaken. My face grew hot as fury and anguish battled for supremacy. It didn't make sense. This kind of stuff wasn't supposed to happen. Not to me.

"Three days." I barely heard his hushed voice. "It's been three days since the accident. I'm sorry...I'm so sorry."

His eyes finally met mine again, but we had nothing to say. My face was expressionless as my brain tried to process his words. I stared around blankly at my surroundings, at me. The metal, there was so much metal. And it hurt, like the ghost of my former flesh haunting me and dragging me into its icy tomb. It itched at the seams. I silently dragged five heavy metal fingers across the blanket spread over my lower body, careful not to snag the IV implanted in my forearm.

With all my strength, I started to force myself out of the bed, and my body immediately gave out as if my muscles were made of jelly. Uncle William jumped up to catch me and helped me lie down again. The weight of the fury coursing through my veins came crashing down, and the only way I knew how to deal with it was to slam my fist into the bed rail. It groaned and screeched as it contorted, and the sounds echoed eerily off the walls.

I screamed in pain and felt tears running down my face. I shrieked, "What did you do to me?!"

Gloom and exhaustion had taken its toll on my uncle. His eyes were filled with sorrow as he tried to control the quiver in his lip. Finally, he sighed, "Wren, you were badly hurt, and you wouldn't have made it.

Your body was so damaged that our only hope to save you was to operate and give you robotic parts, but you're okay now. Remember the robotics I've been working on for a while, something to combine humans and robots?"

"I thought it wasn't ready," I retorted, squinting my eyes accusingly. My breathing slowed and my throat constricted as I realized I was the guinea pig.

"We had no choice." He quickly dug into his shirt pocket for a small mirror and handed it to me. "Look."

The mirror showed my right cheek glazed with sleek metal. I couldn't believe what I was seeing. I already knew my hands had been replaced, but then he showed me the long thin line of metal that crept down my spine and snaked down my legs, ending at my kneecaps. It curled around my legs like leg braces, as opposed to the implanted metal on my face and hands.

I was speechless.

My uncle held out his hand and waited until I placed my metal fingers in his grasp. "It'll be okay," he repeated, "I'm here. I'll take care of you."

I took a few deep breaths.

"Let's just take this one day at a time, okay?" Uncle William sat down close to me.

I shuffled over to lean into his chest, noticing the nerves in my legs were still intact.

After sitting in silence for some time, Uncle William spoke up. "Wren, I found this at the scene." He pulled a glowing object out of his pocket, and his fingers tightened around the strange item for a moment before he opened his hand. It was easy to see he was mesmerized by its beauty. "I'm not sure what it is, but...well..." he whispered, "I don't think it's from this world."

I stared at the tiny blue marble glowing softly in his palm. It looked like the ocean reflecting the sun, shimmering with a million fragments of light. I couldn't look away.

A figure slipped into the room, and out of the corner of my eye, I noticed his smooth golden brown skin and the glare off his glasses that came from the orb's luminescence; however, my focus was locked on the beautiful, mysterious object.

"She's awake." His deep voice was hesitant.

Uncle William discreetly pocketed the orb.

"Have you told her?" the man questioned grimly.

Uncle William responded. "Only what I needed to, Mallick." He then turned to face me. "Wren, this is Rob Mallick. You can call him Mr. Rob. He worked very closely with your father and I...he was a good friend of your father's."

I immediately dropped my gaze at the mention of my dad. I closed my eyes, desperately trying to catch the tears that streamed down my face. My father. My mother. I tried not to think of that day, that day when everything went wrong. But it was too late. I could still hear the screams and the crash of thunder and see the flash of lightning across the sky, and for a moment, I wished I could turn back time.

≋ 12 YEARS, 8 MONTHS, 17 DAYS, 15 HOURS, and 37 MINUTES to SILEO TERRA

September 10, 2057, 8:23 am...

"Wren? Are you coming?" Uncle William whispered. I'd left the door open just a crack, so I opened the door more for him.

My room was not a typical teenager's bedroom. I had set up several desks in all the available space, and my impressive collection of tools and small gadgets littered the room. The walls were covered in blueprints that could have passed for wallpaper.

"Yeah, just changing a battery again. Be out in a sec," I answered, closing the small battery case implanted in the metal of my wrist.

The robotics vastly improved my finger motion and helped me to walk. Although it had been difficult to become accustomed to, it was extraordinary what I was capable of now. Uncle William and I had been constantly updating and improving them for the last five and a half years since the accident.

"We need to hurry. They're waiting for us."

"Well, it's not like they can start without their speaker." I smiled faintly and followed him out, taking in the dull brick walls of the hallway.

The corridors were bare and drab, but each room was filled with supplies and computer screens and different projects, so the window of each door emitted a blue-green glow as we passed by.

I clenched my teeth as we walked, ignoring the butterflies fluttering in my stomach. Uncle William and I had been working on something big.

I remembered Mr. Rob's exact words all those years ago when he had explained what caused the accident, "We were testing the machine and needed to find a suitable power source. We'd discovered it could be powered by flowing electrons in lightning, but when we tested it, we didn't know it would create a time storm, opening a hole into a different dimension for a brief moment. It was as if a black hole was absorbing the sky, but the energy emitted through it was not from this world. That's how we discovered the existence of another dimension. Somehow the storm bent time, and our clocks went haywire. Unfortunately, that was also what caused the accident. The opening allowed the small blue substance to travel here. We believe the orb was drawn to the time storm, and it landed on the road you were travelling on near the facility. Your car was just in the wrong place at the wrong time."

I had completely lost it that day, the news triggering a fit of rage. I hadn't meant to, but I'd just snapped and kept pummelling the wall until the bricks began to crumble.

Nightmares had haunted me every night, and I used to cry a lot but not anymore. Now I controlled it. I no longer allowed my emotions to take me hostage. At first, I'd thought every night about what I could have done differently for my parents to have survived. I had felt so desperate and without hope until one day, the solution became clear in my mind.

What I needed was answers, and the only way to get answers was to travel through time. I had to make sure DAIR's time machine worked.

"You know, Wren, we should name the time machine."

My attention snapped back to the present. I looked up at Uncle William. "We should name it something Latin. Isn't it your favourite language?"

He laughed, "I guess so. I am very fond of it."

"Hmm…so, what's Latin for 'time machine'?"

Uncle William bit his bottom lip and replied, "*Tempus machina.*"

"How about just Tempus? I like that name."

"Me too."

We entered a room filled with two rows of seats facing a transparent wall. Through the wall, we could see our machine covered by a white tarp. Above it was a hole in the towering, dome-shaped ceiling. The whole room was dedicated to time travel. On the left was a metal door that connected the two areas.

I chose a seat in the back on the far left as people started to file in and take their seats around me. They were all agents that formed the government's division of time studies, and they were all dressed identically in formal gray suits and black ties.

I felt extremely out of place. Their eyes were like piercing needles as they stared uncomfortably at my strange metallic robotics.

Uncle William strolled up in front of the group. "First of all, thank you for coming today. I believe we have experienced a major breakthrough in the field of time study." His charming smile made him appear confident and personable all at the same time.

"Time is a mysterious thing," he continued while pacing. "For anything to exist, it must exist within time; in fact, time gives birth to beginnings and determines endings for everything. Think of a child: they grow up, live for a time, and then die. Although time makes existence possible, it also makes the process of aging and death inevitable."

He paused and ran his hand through his hair. "Time will eventually take us all. Dimensions such as height and width and length can all change because of time; however, what if one was to remove oneself from the timeline? Could one travel to another time? Perhaps even another dimension in time? Could one halt the effects of time itself or even reverse the inevitable aging process we all must face? Could it be that immortality is at our fingertips? Vast knowledge might be accumulated in a fraction of a second." He snapped his fingers for emphasis and then continued.

"How would this change the way we currently view the rules of time? Would they still apply? Would it be possible to change events in the past without changing the current timeline? What precautions would we need to take to ensure this? Friends, the possibilities are endless, but so too is the inherent danger. We must concede the possibility that changing the past may have dire consequences as the timeline could be corrupted in a multitude of ways: economies could be sabotaged, technologies could disappear, life-saving inventions might never be invented, and important historical figures and events could cease to have ever existed, plunging our world into anarchy and darkness. Timeline corruption could also unleash all kinds of abnormal natural disasters as the strain on the timeline may cause tectonic plates to shift, volcanoes to erupt, and Mother Nature herself to implode. The list goes on. Even the things that have brought us here today would be in jeopardy." Uncle William paused to let his words sink in.

"But we must also ask whether it is even possible to corrupt the timeline. Does time have the power to correct itself? Or, better yet, do we possess the ability to change what time has already determined? With all this in mind, it is our conviction that future time travel is far less dangerous than past time travel because we simply do not have solid answers to these questions yet, and we cannot afford to risk altering the timeline without these answers. However, we must start somewhere, so it is our recommendation that we begin with the future. Every series of events in the past shapes the present and the future."

Uncle William became more excited as he addressed the logistics of time travel. "We have developed equipment that can notify us of an upcoming time storm, which gives us a slight advantage in preparing for an expedition. A time storm is an irregular, naturally occurring storm where the lightning seems to act as a living creature and is highly reactive. If we could launch the machine using the power created from the lightning discharged from a time storm, it could open up a portal to travel into the dimension that contains the threads of time. We have analyzed the lingering energy from the last time storm and concluded that using a few specific algorithms, we could attach ourselves to a thread. The danger here is that we are unsure if the threads will be altered if we interfere with them, but if our calculations are correct, we should be able to arrive at our desired destination quickly and without incident."

Uncle William stopped to catch his breath and take a sip from his water bottle before continuing yet again. "Think of it as riding on a subway train that travels at speeds far greater than light itself. Travelling on this thread will cause it to become unstable, allowing us to bend it according to our wishes. Our manipulation of the thread will create a shard of time, or a 'station' on the thread, where we will safely arrive at the destination of our choosing. Potentially, we could move forward on a timeline, resulting in a successful expedition to the future."

Mr. Rob interjected in an attempt to clarify, "In short, ladies and gentlemen, we don't just believe time travel is possible, we know it's possible, and we've learned how to control it."

As he opened the floor to questions, I slipped my hand into my pocket and grasped the familiar blue orb. Uncle William usually kept it with him but had given it to me right before walking into the meeting room. I had always sensed he was somewhat reluctant to allow someone else to hold it, so I felt special and important knowing he trusted me with it and only a few people had ever laid eyes on it.

That reminded me that Uncle William had said he was going to introduce me to Mr. Rob's assistant and friend, Alex, soon. Uncle William had said he felt like it was time to tell Alex about the orb, and hopefully, he would be an asset to our project. He had only told me a little bit about Alex's background, but I'd been surprised to hear he was seventeen, just older than me by a year. I was looking forward to having someone my age to talk to.

I stopped listening to the questions, bored with the tedious answers I already knew. Heat radiated in my pocket from the orb. Usually, it was cool to the touch, kind of like the metal on my hands. Now, it seemed as if it was...alive.

Uncle William finished addressing the crowd, turned, and walked through the connecting door. He strode toward the time machine and discarded the tarp, unveiling a metal pyramid with a door that made up almost the entire front panel of the machine. Impenetrable windows were on each side, and the gleaming silver made it look otherworldly. He swung open the door, revealing a single seat facing away from the crowd. The control desk was visible from my seated position, and faint buzzing noises and a glow came from the screen.

Suddenly, a digital voice from the building's intercom announced, "Testing the machine in ten, nine..." Everyone started murmuring around me.

I caught a glimpse of panic on Uncle William's wild-eyed face before he leapt into the machine. He started pressing buttons frantically, but a sudden rumbling beneath our feet caused the door to slam, locking him inside.

"Eight, seven, six..."

I searched for Mr. Rob for answers, but I couldn't see him through the crowd of gray suits, now all standing.

"Five, four, three..."

I rose from my seat. Something had gone wrong. My heart leapt into my throat as I heard faint pounding sounds from behind the time machine's door.

"Two, one..."

This couldn't be for real.

"Zero."

A deep rumbling came from the depths of the time machine, coinciding with the crash of thunder above it. Tremors shook the floor beneath my feet, and a streak of blue light, alive with power, streamed in through the hole above the time machine. However, it didn't just strike the pointed tip of the machine like it should have but also veered toward the door connecting the two rooms.

I shoved my hand into my pocket only to find a small round hole. The orb was gone! I realized it must have burned a hole in my pocket, and because of my robotics, I wouldn't have felt the heat on that part of my leg. Desperately scanning the floor, I finally saw it rolling toward the other room. The lightning and the orb—they were attracted to each other. I dove onto the floor and grabbed the orb before it got to the door, but that didn't stop the lightning. The blue lightning blew the connecting door to smithereens as I lay there, covering my head with my arms. I looked around, disoriented from the blast.

Screams drew my attention to the other side of the transparent wall where Uncle William, inside the time machine, was surrounded by lightning. Tempus was ablaze. I leapt to my feet and screamed, "Uncle!" but my voice was drowned out in the sudden fierce wind.

I ran toward the time machine, but the lightning jumped from the machine to me. It weaved through my fingers, tingling and tickling rather than hurting me, and flickered against the orb. In a panic, I threw the orb to the floor, and then everything exploded.

The violent blast propelled me against the wall, and as suddenly as it had all begun, it ended. There was only silence. I couldn't move, but I could open my eyes. The orb sat in front of me glowing its usual blue, both mesmerizing and terrifying. I slowly reached out and grabbed it. Clenching it in my metal fist, I turned my gaze to the machine, but it wasn't there. Tempus was no more. The explosion had completely destroyed it, and all that was left were small jagged pieces of the shell scattered on the ground. The lightning, now also glowing a deep, brilliant blue, returned through the hole in the roof and vanished.

No, not again.

I could hear someone questioning Mr. Rob outside the room.

"What do we do?"

"I have no idea. There's no explanation for that explosion. The machine wasn't even supposed to be turned on."

"What about her?"

"She has to stay here, she has nowhere to go."

"For how long, Mallick?"

Silence. All the conversations concerning me since Tempus had blown up yesterday had ended like this.

I slumped against the door. I was in Uncle William's workspace. Cluttered papers and half-finished designs filled all the available space. If that wasn't messy enough, I had all my supplies stored haphazardly in one corner.

Surprisingly, I hadn't been injured too severely, just a few cuts and burn marks. I suppose I should have been grateful, but I sure didn't feel like it. The pain on the outside was minimal compared to the inside.

Uncle William hadn't planned on turning anything on yesterday. He knew the machine wasn't ready to be tested. The presentation had only been meant to secure more funding for the project. What had happened? What had gone wrong? And beyond that, why had it blown up instead of just jumping to another time? I had no answers. The orb had somehow triggered the explosion and messed things up. Now there was no Uncle William, and there was no Tempus.

I picked up the nearest table and hurled it in frustration. It collided with the wall with a thud, and its contents clattered to the ground. Dragging my metallic fingers through my hair, I clutched the orb in my pants pocket. I knew what to do and I needed Mr. Rob. Though I wouldn't admit it—and didn't even know how to ask for it—I needed his help. I needed Uncle William. I needed my parents. Tears began to well up in my eyes.

Slamming my fist against the wall, I released some of the storm brewing inside of me. The clang echoed in my ears. Sinking to my knees, I curled up in a ball and tried to shrink away.

⇛ 12 YEARS, 8 MONTHS, 9 DAYS, 6 HOURS, and 26 MINUTES to SILEO TERRA

September 18, 2057, 5:34 pm...

"I have to do it. I have to rebuild the time machine."

Mr. Rob's dark eyes stared at me; he wasn't sure how to reply. We were in my room, sitting across from each other at a cluttered table. Uncle William's blueprints for Tempus were laid out in front of us.

Mr. Rob sighed and took off his glasses, rubbing his eyes in frustration. "Wren, what you need is help to overcome your grief. It's only been a week since William's death. You need people to help you work through the trauma in your past. There are people in this building that specialize in that."

"This is what I need." I smoothed out the blueprints and set the orb in between us.

Mr. Rob muttered, "I don't know."

He reached for the orb, but I snatched it away.

"This is the answer," I insisted, cradling the orb. "This is the last part of my uncle I have left. This is all I have left. You can't take it away." My eyes grew teary until everything in my room started to blur together. I wiped my eyes and looked up at Mr. Rob. He looked defeated. "Mr. Rob, I need supplies. You have to understand that this is what I want, and this is what I need."

Mr. Rob bit his lip. "Okay, okay," he said gently. "For now, you do whatever you need to do, and when you're ready to listen to me and talk to other people—there is a life outside your room, you know—you let me know." Mr. Rob inhaled deeply. "Deal?"

I nodded and smiled, wrapping my fingers around the pulsing orb; Tempus would live again.

⇛ 10 YEARS, 7 MONTHS, 26 DAYS, 8 HOURS, and 52 MINUTES to SILEO TERRA

October 1, 2059, 3:08 pm...

This was my daily routine: wake up, work, build, study, eat, build, work, study, eat, scream in a fit of rage, bang on the walls, talk to Mr. Rob, work harder with no intention of ever stopping to sleep, fall asleep anyway. Repeat. That had been my life for the last two years. I didn't remember much of anything else. My life before the accident felt like a vague memory, a dream from long ago.

Fingering the orb in one hand, I carefully screwed hinges on the door of Tempus II with the other. It was almost finished, but would it work?

I opened the door and placed the orb on the control desk. The computer analyzed it immediately. POWER SOURCE appeared on the screen. Accessing the keyboard, I brought up a digital image of the lightning trigger. The trigger's purpose was to convert the lightning into usable energy that would hold open the dimension, allowing us to access the threads of time. The trigger had also been the part that had malfunctioned last time; however, this time, I had added a nice spot to place the orb below the pointed tip.

I propped up a ladder against the side of the pyramid-shaped machine and climbed up to check that the trigger was securely in place. There was no doubt in my mind the lighting would strike it this time. I climbed down the ladder and jumped to the floor, surprised by the hope and excitement growing inside me.

I scarcely left my room anymore unless I needed food or had to meet with my tutor. Most things I needed I just kept in my room—I had moved out the extra desks to make space for Tempus II. Blueprints still papered the walls, but now, they all were associated with rebuilding the time machine. Since DAIR couldn't exactly drop me off at the nearest orphanage with these robotic parts of mine, I was allowed to remain, tinkering and building and creating. One of the only times I left this room was to walk with Mr. Rob; otherwise, he would just come see me in my room.

A knock on the door jolted me out of my thoughts, and I quickly slipped the orb into my pocket before opening the door. I expected it to be Mr. Rob, but I hesitated when I saw a lady dressed in a dark frumpy pantsuit beside him. Her low ponytail was pulled back tightly, making her bird-like features look even sharper. The serious expression on her face was a fitting accessory for her overall look. Her lips pursed together tightly in a slight frown.

"Good afternoon, Wren. This is Ms. Quinn, and she has been instructed to examine your workplace."

"Why?" I asked suspiciously.

"Safety, health, etcetera," Ms. Quinn replied curtly. Her exceptionally long, pointed nose made her look snooty. She peered down at me, and I sensed the air of superiority that engulfed her. It made the hair on my neck bristle, and I suppressed the anger that rushed to the surface.

"Give me a second," I grumbled and shut the door more roughly than I had meant to.

A large safe sat under the table at the back of the room, and I quickly chucked the orb in and locked it up. I tidied up a little as I casually walked back to the door. I didn't mind making them wait. As I reopened the door, Ms. Quinn impatiently pushed past, and Mr. Rob waved me over to him.

"Need some fresh air?" he asked gently, his eyes glancing down the hallway.

I nodded. He led me through the labyrinth of the complex. I looked over at him and made note of how confident he always looked. He was taller than most people, but he never slouched.

We approached a security guard at the main doors. This particular guard had icy blue eyes and never had anything nice to say. I looked away as Mr. Rob walked up to him.

The guard looked at his watch. "You have fifteen minutes before she needs to come back inside," he grumbled and waved his hand dismissively.

Mr. Rob and I walked out of the building, matching each other's strides. I took a deep breath and welcomed the cool, crisp air that flooded into my lungs. Autumn had arrived, and the air was wonderfully chilly. The sky was a dreary gray; enormous clouds masked the normal intensity of the sun as it made its way toward the horizon.

I expected one of our usual chats, but Mr. Rob looked like he was deep in thought.

After a while, I broke the silence. "So, Mr. Rob, what's on your mind?"

He looked down at me and smiled warmly. "Wren, I think you're old enough now you can just call me Rob."

"That's what was on your mind?"

He gave a short laugh but seemed to be choosing his next words carefully. "Wren, do you remember the last time you were out here? Outside?"

How long had it been? I frequently lost track of time. I replied nonchalantly, "Oh, it has to have been a couple of days, right?"

Rob sighed and mumbled, "It's been a week and a half."

I noted the concern in his tone and stared at him blankly. "Wasn't that far off though," I said lightly. "I've been working a lot lately. I got the parts I was waiting for, and I think I'm getting close."

"Do you even remember how long you've been living here?"

"Yeah, but it's all okay with me. I don't expect to ever leave," I answered and then smirked. "Except through the time machine."

"Nearly eight years."

"That sounds right. You told me I was turning eighteen soon."

"*Eight* years." He looked comical when his features were stern and his brows furrowed. Rob stared at me for a few seconds before looking off into the distance. "That's too long. You are my responsibility and I've let you down. I'm sorry I haven't helped you the way you needed to be helped. You should be living a healthy, normal life. You should be healing from your grief. We should have helped you reintegrate into the outside world. You know, like going to regular school instead of getting tutors."

I stiffened at the mention of regular school and grumbled, "I've gone through more tutors than I can count because I'm smarter than all of them, and they treat me like I'm a kid."

A moment of silence passed. Then, when I thought we were done, he continued, "We aren't sure what to do with you. I've been debating whether to tell them about the orb. I just don't know." Frustrated, he removed his glasses and massaged his temple. "Maybe it would be best if other people looked at it. I know William didn't want the other members of the organization to know of it at the time, but we could make it a new project. William certainly must not have wanted to hide it for this long." He sighed again. "To be clear, I'm asking you to give it up. Let other...professionals handle it. I'm sure William would have understood. I only let you keep it because that's what he told me he wanted if anything happened to him—to keep it safe I mean; not necessarily to let you hide it. You shouldn't feel like you're trapped here. You're not a child anymore. Let's talk about what direction you'd like to go in. "

"I don't want them to take it. I need it. It's mine...my uncle's. I will never give it up." Glaring at Rob, I seized his arm. "Don't do anything, please. I'm fine."

I was surprised to see shock reflected in his eyes.

"Wren?" Rob's voice was shaky. "What happened?" His face paled. "Your eyes turned bright blue."

"Sorry." I released my grasp and staggered back, disoriented from the peculiar pressure in my head. "I don't know what came over me. Just a little tired today, I guess."

With his sleeve, Rob wiped away the sweat that beaded across his forehead. "I'm sorry, Wren. I've made up my mind." He turned his back and stepped away in a hurry.

I raced past him. I was faster and stronger, and I wasn't going to let him take it. He yelled for me to stop but I couldn't. Even though he was sprinting as fast as he could to keep up with me, I beat him back to the building by a long shot.

I ran straight to my room, weaving around a few people and dodging a surprised Ms. Quinn right outside my door. Locking it, I listened as the fast-paced clicking of her heels faded. I bent down and allowed myself to catch my breath, but only for a second.

Thundering knocks came from the door, and Rob's concerned voice echoed through. "Wren, open the door. Please listen to me. The orb is not safe, and I'm afraid it's hurting you." I knew I couldn't keep him out forever. I needed a plan. But first, I had to get the orb.

The pounding at the door paused. I froze, trying to hear what he was doing. Suddenly, a strong gust of wind whipped my hair across my face. Wind? As I looked around, papers and tools began spinning and whipping into the corners of the room. Tables toppled over and slid along the ground. I grabbed one and used it to steady myself. I looked around in confusion. I blinked my eyes as I noticed the ceiling rippling like it was made of liquid.

Despite the howling wind, I heard clicking. Someone was trying to pick the lock. I gritted my teeth, but I didn't look away from the ceiling. Slowly, the liquid-like surface turned dark. A black hole appeared in the ceiling, and then even more slowly, a large, rectangular metal machine started descending through the hole. A scream wrenched out of my throat. Maybe Rob was right. Maybe I did need some serious help if I was starting to experience such vivid hallucinations.

All movement around me came to a stop as time slowed down...and finally froze. Papers hung in mid-air, and my trusty ladder that had been propped up against Tempus II now hovered above me, eerily hanging in suspense.

The machine touched down. Its door unlatched, revealing a rugged man. Even though shadows hid most of the details of his face, I could still make out his intense expression. I continued blinking my eyes, hoping to wake myself up.

He stepped forward and stared at me for a few long seconds before speaking. "Wren Derecho?"

I didn't move. I didn't make a sound. His piercing hazel eyes were terrifying.

"Don't be scared. My name is Donahue, and we've come from your current future. 2070 to be exact."

"Am I dreaming?" My whispered question was directed to myself rather than to the stranger.

"No, you're not dreaming." He exhaled slowly. "Wren, we desperately need your help. Your future is not a particularly good one. When you combine the orb with the time machine, it merges with your robotics. You become the most powerful person on the planet, but it takes control of you. Harnessing the orb's power, you create a 'perfect city' out of the city of Ashborne. In an attempt to eliminate all threats and potential danger, you end up taking away all freedom to achieve strict order. We believe you are the only one who can stop yourself. We need your help."

Clouds swirled around in my brain. I gawked at him and tried to steady my voice. "No, actually, I'm going insane. I'm the one who needs help. So, thanks for the offer, but I'm going to take a hard pass."

Donahue nodded and looked at me for a few seconds. "Where's the orb, Wren?"

"Wha-what? What are you, um…talking about?" Naturally, my eyes darted to the safe.

He walked over to the safe, and I lunged to stop him, but he clasped onto my wrist with an iron grip, holding me at arms' length. I tried to wrench my hand away, but he was surprisingly strong.

With his other hand, he pulled out a navy-blue, pistol-like weapon with a long barrel. I stopped struggling and held my breath, my body tense with fear.

"Ever heard of a VU?" he asked, almost sadly. "Don't worry, I won't use it on you."

Donahue pointed the weapon toward the safe and pulled the trigger. I watched in amazement as the strange weapon zapped the safe's lock and melted a hole right through the door. The lump of molten metal oozed onto the floor, and the safe door swung open. When he saw the glowing orb, his grip loosened slightly, and I wriggled free and snatched the orb up before he had a chance.

"Wren, I need you to cooperate."

I looked down at the orb in my hand and shoved it in my pocket.

He grabbed my arm again and began to drag me toward his machine. I screamed and tried to wrench my arm out of his grasp. When I tried to punch him with my free hand, he twisted his body so I only barely connected with his elbow. He winced and clenched his jaw, yet he didn't loosen his grip. I lost my balance and fell to my knees. Still he didn't stop dragging me. I slammed my fist into the back of one leg to slow him down, and to my surprise, a familiar clang filled my ears.

"What are you?" I asked. Cold dread filled my body.

"The same as you," he replied as a twisted grin grew on his face.

⮑? YEARS, ? MONTHS, ? DAYS, ? HOURS, and ? MINUTES to SILEO TERRA

Unknown date, unknown time...

"**D**onahue, hurry up!" A slim woman with jet black hair exclaimed from within the machine. By her side was another guy, his features the opposite of hers, with his blonde hair and bulky figure.

The blonde man stared at me and remarked, "Vee, she's identical to her. What a trip!" The girl ignored him.

Donahue, still clutching my arm, muttered through his clenched teeth, "Tolli, help me."

As Donahue forced me inside with Tolli's assistance, I tried to choke Donahue with my free hand. My robotics may have given me incredible superhuman strength, but eventually, all three of them pinned me down until I stopped fighting. Donahue shoved me into a chair bolted to the floor, keeping his hand on my wrist as he sat down next to me. The woman they called Vee went to the control desk.

"Where are we going?" I demanded. My head was spinning from the sudden events as I tried to make sense of what had just happened.

Vee responded without looking away from the screens, "We're in the dimension that holds the threads of time, and we're heading toward our present, your future."

I studied my captors. It was three against one. Not fair at all. Tolli was now leaning against the desk, watching Vee work but glancing at me every few seconds. Donahue refused to look at me but kept a firm grip on my wrist in case I decided to fight again. Mysteriously, he had similar robotics to me, except his were mostly on his legs; the brace-like robotics looked like they also helped him walk. Metal laced the fingers on his left hand—the hand he had used to grab me—so he had an iron grip that rivalled mine. I wondered what had happened to him.

Sighing, I looked around at the interior of the time machine; it was much more advanced than mine. Everything was stark white, and small lights were set into the ceiling, dimly illuminating my captors.

Donahue finally met my eyes. There was a bright red mark across his neck from where I had grabbed him. He glared at me. It was unsettling, but understandable, so I looked away.

The view out the window was breathtaking. The threads of time reminded me of outer space but had more vibrant colours that looked like twisting veins of bright purples and blues; they shimmered and danced as we sped by. I was captivated by their beauty.

Throbbing pressure started pounding in my skull, and the uneasy feeling of motion sickness began to take hold of my stomach. I had known this would happen if I ever travelled to the future. Burning bile surged in the back of my throat. Taking deep breaths, I looked around for a distraction.

Tolli turned to me. "We have limited time for you to change the future. Right now, your present is frozen, but after time runs out, everything will change for either good or bad."

Donahue shook his head at Tolli, obviously wanting him to stay silent.

"I have no idea what you're talking about, and as you may be able to tell, I've never been to the future before," I remarked sarcastically.

Tolli laughed, the sides of his blue eyes crinkling. "Well, it's like if we set a bowl of ice cream on the counter. Soon, it won't be frozen anymore." He rubbed his stomach while he talked about ice cream. "If you wait long enough, it will be completely inedible. So just pretend our time left is that ice cream."

"Our time left?"

"Tolli," Donahue interjected, leaning forward and letting go of my wrist.

Tolli didn't seem to hear him. "Man, there are some really cool things in the future. You'll see once we get there. You helped improve our technology a lot, well…er, you will. Or maybe you already have." Tolli scratched the top of his head. "Time travelling is scrambling my brain."

A slight smile appeared on my face against my will. Out of these three, Tolli seemed the friendliest.

"Do you kidnap people a lot? You actually seem like a pretty nice guy," I said.

"No, you're special, Wren. And we're kinda in a time crunch."

His gaze wandered around the small space, deep in thought. "You know, I witnessed the development of the bubble shield that now surrounds our city. Nothing comes in and nothing comes out except you. The orb found you, it ended up in your hands, and everything went downhill after that. Finally, after all these years, we have a chance to stop you before it's too late…so we have to do it before the ice cream melts!"

I instinctively clasped my hands together on my lap and thought of how I was going to convince them they had the wrong person.

Then a puzzling thought crossed my mind. "How do you guys know about the orb?"

"Everybody knows about it in our time," he replied.

Vee announced, "Preparing to drop."

"Wait, what?" I felt my eyes bulge out of their sockets. "Drop where?"

Donahue, who had been studying me the entire time, suddenly spoke up. "You always were full of questions."

We began to descend, causing my stomach to lurch into my throat. I clenched my teeth together so hard, I was sure they would shatter.

⇶ 1 DAY, 3 HOURS, and 23 MINUTES to SILEO TERRA

May 26, 2070, 8:37 pm...

My eyelids fluttered open, and I strained to see in the dim light. I wasn't in the machine anymore, but rather, I was lying on a hard mattress with my head propped up on a pillow. Something was amiss as I looked around, and the clock on the wall confirmed it; it didn't match my internal clock. The last five hours couldn't have simply disappeared.

Vee poked her head through the doorway and noticed I was awake. She approached me reluctantly. "Comfy?"

"Definitely. Never better." I flashed a fake, sarcastic grin. "My head is spinning like a top, and if I get up, I'll probably throw up. Where—when—am I?"

"This is where we call home now that...that...oh, never mind. It's 2070. Almost 11 years in your future. But don't worry, you can rest for a while. You won't be going anywhere tonight," she replied.

I scowled, "What do you guys want from me?" I just couldn't wrap my mind around all of this. Was I supposed to fight for these people or something? I wanted answers, but a small part of me also dreaded finding out.

"Um...well, Donahue wanted to explain things to you, but I guess I could tell you a little bit. First, we're going to have to get to Ashborne, after we set up the device—oh! Yes, the shield. Have to pass through that and find the office tower...but we can't be recognized, and—"

I held up a hand in protest. "Too much." I massaged my forehead and sighed, "This is too much."

"Well, you'll find out all the specifics soon enough. Lay still; you'll feel better in a moment." Vee disappeared in an instant and Tolli casually strode in.

"You know, we're the good guys here."

"You're all just afraid of me," I retorted. "Everyone is."

"No, we just need some time to build trust. You're a different person in our time."

"But you need something from me. So it's my trust, not yours, that's wanted." Although I was still dizzy and disoriented, I made myself sit up.

"Okay, well first, we need your trust, so you agree to join us on our mission. Then, I need you to *try* to work nicely with the others and gain their trust. You're not exactly a good person in this timeline. Oh, and just a helpful hint, don't call Donahue 'Donna.' He despises that. Brings back bad memories." Tolli paused dramatically. "Anyway, I trust you," he said with a grin and a wink.

I smiled at him with a real smile this time. "Thanks."

"Need water? Food?"

I groaned as I slowly rose. Tolli extended his hand and I took it.

"Maybe you should stay still for a few more minutes."

I shook my head; I was already feeling a lot better than I had when I'd first woken up.

Vee returned and gestured for me to follow her. We left Tolli whistling softly to himself.

She briefly explained we were in an abandoned warehouse that went a few levels underground. It was obvious it was only the four of us here, so I figured I could make an easy escape. All I needed now was a place to go.

Vee helped me down the cracked concrete steps with a hand on my back. One level below, on the ground floor, she explained, "Kitchen's down the hall. The bathroom is to our right."

Vee pointed out a large, meticulously organized room to our left. "This is where we work. It rarely looks this clean, but I tidied up since we were expecting company." I didn't acknowledge her joke but took a quick look around. Too bad I didn't see anything useful.

I started feeling dizzy again, and Vee must have noticed my face turning pale.

"You need something to eat to regain your energy. And you need to sit down." She pivoted on her heels in one swift, smooth motion, turning the opposite way. I tried to scramble after her, and we ended up in the small kitchen at the end of the hallway. I plopped down onto a chair at the small wooden table in the middle of the room and rested my head on my arms as I watched Vee open the fridge.

She met my eyes and immediately looked away.

"What do you want?" Her voice was strained.

"Anything."

Vee grabbed a premade sandwich from the refrigerator and placed it in front of me. She poured a cup of coffee for herself and looked up to see if I wanted a cup also. I made a face and shook my head, and then I unwrapped the sandwich as fast as I could.

Vee waited until I finished eating to speak, "Before you disappeared, we were really good friends." Beneath the curt comment and serious expression on her face, she sounded sad. "I thought you were dead. I thought I would never see you again." A single tear ran down her face before she swiped it away. "I couldn't believe it when I saw you again; so many years had passed by already. I was overjoyed. But you must not have felt the same way, or you wouldn't have done what you did. Sometimes I'm glad you eventually forgot about us, our friendship."

Vee exhaled loudly, "Sorry, you have no idea what I'm talking about. You probably don't even remember me."

I stared at her. She did look familiar, now that I studied her face, with her gray eyes and short straight hair slightly curled in at her chin.

I hadn't allowed myself to think about my life before the crash. It had hurt too much. My mind raced, and I was transported back to the day of the accident. I clasped my hands over my ears to drown out the sounds of reverberating thunder and the screams that threatened to viciously shred my brain from the inside out.

Vee placed her hand on my shoulder, and the touch pulled me out of my vivid memory.

I looked up. I remembered her face. I remembered a little girl...

⇛ 18 YEARS, 5 MONTHS, 3 DAYS, 8 HOURS, and 30 MINUTES to SILEO TERRA

December 24, 2051, 3:30 pm...

Cassandra Viola giggled, "I love making snow angels."

"I love not going to school, Cass," I snickered, enjoying the freshly fallen snow with Cass in her backyard.

Ever since she'd moved down the street a year ago, we had been inseparable. It was so fun having a friend live close by, even though we were in different grades. Now that it was Christmas break, we had lots of time to spend together.

"Why? School is fun!" She jumped up and slipped again, plopping down in the snow.

"Nah, too many people."

"Right." She beamed, crinkling her gray eyes.

Cass was a friend to all, and everyone loved her. That's why it was so easy to be around her.

"Anyway," she perked up, "I was wondering, what do you want to be when you grow up?"

I shrugged in response. Cass was also very curious and asked lots of questions, but surprisingly, she never made me feel uncomfortable.

Cass continued without missing a beat, "I want to be an astronaut or maybe a scientist."

I waddled over to her in my baggy snow pants and looked up at her under my oversized toque.

"You'll figure it out too, Wren. You always do."

≡ 1 DAY, 2 HOURS, and 29 MINUTES to SILEO TERRA

May 26, 2070, 9:31 pm...

If I truly wanted to work through the trauma of my past, I knew I needed to let the pain in. Rob had told me that once. However, I wasn't quite ready for that, so I pushed the floating thoughts of my childhood away and focused on the girl sitting across from me in this new time, almost twenty years after that Christmas Eve.

I leaned closer to her. "Cass?" Her body grew tense. "You loved to play in the snow."

With tears glistening in her eyes, she nodded. She stood up abruptly and whispered hoarsely, "Sorry, I guess I'm not quite ready for this."

Without glancing back, Cass left me to my thoughts. I dropped my eyes to the floor in confusion. I looked at my hands and noticed they needed some repairs. Instinctively, I slipped them into my pockets and felt the calmness flow through my body as my fingers closed around the orb. It was the only thing I understood.

I sighed and rose from the table. I needed to accept there was no one in this world who could understand me. I didn't follow Cass. Instead, I headed in the other direction, down another hall.

Even though I was utterly exhausted, I didn't want to find my way back to my bed yet. As I came to the end of the hall, I saw a room to my right that looked like it might have some tools. Good enough. I walked in and saw a rusty toolbox in the corner. I opened it up and pulled out a screwdriver. Then I searched for some kind of power source. Did they even use batteries in the future? I picked up a glowing cylinder, similar in shape to what I needed.

Tolli suddenly appeared at the door. "You really shouldn't mess with that stuff," he warned.

I jumped, dropping the object on the table. "Do you have any batteries?"

"Yeah, in the museum," he chuckled. Tolli snatched up the cylinder I'd dropped. "This is part of a weapon." I winced and then he added, "Nothing too dangerous. We're limited, thanks to you." Grabbing something more resembling a battery from a different compartment, he tossed it to me and remarked, "Here, use this. You may need to eventually find a different power source though. Batteries are pretty scarce around here. The kind you need, anyway."

We walked out of the room and he turned to me. "Ya good?"

"Yeah, I think I'll just go back to my room now," I replied and tried to walk away, but he followed me. We silently walked up a flight of stairs before we came upon a lone figure leaning against the wall in the stairwell.

Donahue's expression was stoic, and he nodded at Tolli in acknowledgement. His metal flashed with each move, reflecting the moonlight coming in through a window. He joined us as we continued up the steps.

"Why do you need *me* here?" I asked him, breaking the silence. The sooner I helped them with whatever they needed, the sooner I would get to go home. I needed to escape this place as soon as possible.

"We can get to all of that tomorrow, Wren."

"But what about being in a time crunch? The melting ice cream?" I argued.

"We're not exactly sure how long—"

I interrupted, "And if I can't do what you want me to do?"

"I—"

"Do you even care about what happens to me?"

"Of course," Donahue pressed his dark lips together, then replied, "but we have a mission…it is imperative we complete it."

A sudden burst of anger rose up in my chest and exploded out of me and I shouted, "BUT WHAT ABOUT ME? WHAT ABOUT WHAT I WANT? I WANT TO GO HOME!"

Donahue and Tolli stopped in their tracks and exchanged worried glances. Donahue hesitantly placed his hand on my shoulder. "Wren, you need to calm down."

"I'm fine. Just get out of my way." I shrugged his hand off my shoulder and tried to shove my way past him, but my effort was weak.

I must have looked fragile because Donahue raised his hands up and softened his expression. "You're obviously tired, and it may be difficult for you to grasp some of the things we need to discuss. Let me walk you back to your room."

I was exhausted, but I didn't want to give him the satisfaction of being right. "Sure. You look like you need some rest too, Donna."

Donahue didn't reply but turned to glare at Tolli, who responded with a shrug and stifled a laugh. I decided to shut my mouth.

The three of us started walking down the short hallway at the top of the stairs, but Donahue blocked Tolli.

"I can take her to her room."

Tolli shot him a suspicious look but didn't say anything as he gave a quick salute and turned around.

As much as I wanted to snap at Donahue and tell him I didn't need his help, I bit my tongue. Awkward silence lingered between us as we made our way to my room. If Donahue had wanted to talk to me about something, he must have changed his mind because when we got there, he stopped for a only brief second before turning to walk away. "Try to get some rest, Wren."

"Hold on," I called out, desperate for some answers. "Why am I not supposed to call you Donna?"

He turned around to look at me and cocked his head to one side, "You just can't hold off on the questions, can you?" He still wasn't smiling, but I detected a slight sense of amusement in his voice.

I tried again, "Okay, well if you don't want to answer that question, at least tell me what you want me to call you."

He hesitated before answering, "Alex."

"What?"

"That's my name, Alex Donahue."

And just like that, the puzzle pieces fell into place.

≡ PART TWO ≡
ALEX DONAHUE

≋ 17 YEARS, 9 MONTHS, 16 DAYS, 2 HOURS, and 53 MINUTES to SILEO TERRA

August 11, 2052, 9:07 pm...

The thirst was unbearable, and the hunger consumed my every thought. I hated the empty pit in my stomach, not because of the pain, but because it reminded me that I had nothing in this world, nothing at all. The shaggy curls in my black hair were matted with dirt and sweat but my appearance didn't bother me. Boys my age—twelve, thirteen, I didn't really remember anymore—didn't care about that stuff, especially when they had more important things to worry about. My caramel brown skin had darkened even more with all the time I spent in the hot sun, and I could still feel the heat even though the day was almost done. I looked down at the holes in my shirt—if you could call these rags a shirt—and saw that my ribs were becoming visible. I was small and scrawny for my age, and my face was nothing special to look at, but my nose never failed me.

Behind me, the sun was setting in an array of vivid colours, and I became aware of the savoury aroma of roasting meat filling my nostrils and causing my stomach to rumble like a thunderstorm. I followed the tantalizing smell. It led me past dead trees whose branches stretched out to grab me like bony claws. I flinched when a branch roughly scraped my shoulder, but the delicious smells urged me on. Busy looking around, I accidentally bumped into a wooden ladder and it almost toppled over. The owner of the ladder was fixing a hole on top of his scrap-metal roof and leaned over to scold me loudly as I raced away.

I was getting close to the source of the smell. I had just begun to pick up my pace when suddenly a woman with a pale blue scarf around her head stepped into my path and shoved a heavy basket into my stomach.

"Oof. Sorry, Miss Dogra."

Miss Dogra had been giving me chores occasionally in exchange for the odd hot meal. As I turned to leave, she grabbed my arm. She looked suspiciously at me with tired black eyes. I noticed her hair had started to turn gray when her scarf slipped down to her shoulder.

Miss Dogra commanded, "Boy, take this basket to that house across the street." In a flash, her short figure vanished back inside her house, and I was left to lug the heavy basket of patched clothing across the dusty street.

After I finished the errand, it didn't take me long to find exactly what my nose was leading me to, for even before the house came into view, I could hear waves of laughter coming from what must have been a party. A plump middle-aged man swung open the front door and left it partially open as he carelessly sauntered away. I took this as an invitation to slide right in. I cautiously entered, relieved to find none of the tipsy guests had noticed me. The men all looked like they had completed a hard day's work, with their rough hands and tired eyes. They wore identical looks of exhaustion the alcohol only partially masked. The women wore long colourful dresses with sleeves that brushed their delicate elbows and hems that hung low enough to hide their sandaled feet. Some had scarves wrapped around their dark hair. Even though no one was truly rich in our village in comparison to the world's standards, to me, they were the richest people around. I stayed in the shadows, as that was always the safest place to be, and silently slipped under the table.

The guests kept laughing and chattering away. One man almost kicked me as he shifted in his seat, but I nimbly ducked under the errant kick. I had done this many times before in my young life, and my hands moved swiftly and stealthily to steal a piece of bread off a tray on the table I was hiding under. I shoved it in my mouth and gulped down the delicious morsel. Immediately, the pain in my belly began to subside, but my nose was yelling at my stomach, telling it that something more satisfying was available. The aroma of the meat was overpowering, and I peeked out to see if I could get even the smallest taste. I slowly raised my eyes to see what my nose had led me to, but the moment I saw where the meat was, my heart sank. It was on a table in the middle of the next room and was surrounded by guests. I couldn't risk getting caught as stealing was a major offence in our village, and I had witnessed firsthand the terrible retribution.

I knew I couldn't stay much longer, so I popped out from under the table, grabbed another piece of bread, and darted for the exit.

As I ran down the dusty road lined with dilapidated bicycles and scattered trash, the only sound I could hear was the flapping of hanging laundry caught in the slight breeze. The constant dryness in my throat sent me into a coughing fit. Bent over coughing, but still trying to run, I bumped into something. Startled, I jumped back. It was a man, one who stood out in our village with his pale skin and tailored clothes. His blonde hair fell over his slightly damp forehead, and his pale blue eyes sparkled, making his smile appear genuine.

He had a water bottle in his hand and was trying to talk to me, but I didn't understand what he was saying. After I shook my head, he pointed to his water. I nodded.

The man placed the water on the ground and stepped back. I picked it up and gulped it all down while keeping an eye on him. I couldn't remember the last time I'd had clean water to drink. It was glorious!

As I finished, another man joined us. His features were like mine, with his brown skin and black wavy hair. Round glasses perched on the tip of his hooked nose, highlighting his thin face and strong jawline. However, the most striking difference between us was that his cheeks and eyes were not sunken from hunger and malnutrition like mine. His mouth turned up into a gentle smile as he gazed down at me. Stumbling backward, I raised my hands. I didn't want any trouble.

"Hey, it's okay, little guy." He spoke in my language.

I stared at him.

"Where are your parents?"

Panic suddenly consumed me, and before he could continue, I turned and sprinted away. I didn't stop until I got home.

Home was outside the village. It was a ragged little shack with a roof of straw and mud and walls haphazardly put together with whatever we could find: bits of wood, straw, paper, and metal, all held together with mud and clay. And I loved it.

My parents used to live here too, but they were gone now. Flopping on the ground to catch my breath, I thought about Mama and Baba. I remembered when Mama used to let me sleep beside her and when Baba would sit me down to tell me stories. Now I was all alone.

20 YEARS, 11 MONTHS, 2 DAYS, and 19 HOURS to SILEO TERRA

June 25, 2049, 5:00 am...

"Baba, tell me a bedtime story," I said sleepily as I cuddled in his warm, strong arms.

It was cold tonight, and Baba had just come home from a hard day's work. Mama was sleeping beside us, wrapped in old rags.

"My boy, there's nothing I wouldn't do for you." He smiled, flashing his crooked teeth, and in his gruff voice he began, "There once was a little prince, much like you, who lived in a grand palace with tons of food. Meats, pitas, rice, lemons, you name it, more food than you or I could imagine."

I licked my dry, cracked lips as Baba continued, "But his parents, the king and queen, were not very concerned with their kingdom's people. The people were slowly starving, and the young prince's heart hurt for them. He snuck food from the palace and shared it with the people. They thanked him quietly for his gift of generosity. When the king and queen found out, they got very angry. They disowned him and threw him out on the street."

I closed my eyes, imagining myself as the young prince thrown out on the streets.

Baba pulled me so close to his chest, I could hear his heartbeat. Baba wasn't a gentle man, but he still made me feel safe and loved. "But do you know what that young prince did? He worked very hard to get food, and when he did get some pita or rice, he would still share it with the people. Except now, the people thanked him loudly for his gift of generosity. You see, my boy, even the most unlikely people can do great things. No one thought the poor young prince could have helped the village people, but he gave them what he had. Every person has something to give. Use the gifts you have been given and share them with others. Use them for good."

"I will," I promised, drifting off to sleep.

"I know you will, son."

"Mama, where is Baba going?" I asked. Mama held me close. Tears pooled in her eyes and spilled over, and I wondered why there was no end to the stream that left streaks on her dusty cheeks.

I pointed to Baba, who was being led away by armed soldiers, but she didn't answer. They soon became obscure figures in the early morning sun. It was so bright, I had to look away.

"Mama?" I asked, puzzled about the situation I was witnessing.

She responded by pulling me in closer and remained silent for a moment before saying in a shaky, mournful whisper, "Baba has to go now."

I didn't understand. Once, Mama had told me I had two older brothers who'd also had to leave, but I didn't remember them. Now, the same thing was happening to Baba.

"I know you don't understand, my boy. Sometimes I don't either. What I do know is there are bad people in this world, but it's important not to let the bad people and negative experiences keep you from seeing the good in those around you. If you lose sight of the fact that even the most undesirable of people can find redemption, then you've lost your way. Sometimes people can make very bad decisions and mistakes in life that lead them down the wrong path, but don't give up on them too soon. You need to give them a chance."

Her words went over my head, but they were not lost on me as later in life these words of wisdom would shape me and give me hope even when things seemed hopeless. However, right now, her words didn't make sense, and I didn't want to bother her with any more questions, so I hugged her close. She sighed and pushed back my thick hair so she could look me in the eyes. "I know you're only eight years old, but my boy, you will do great things one day. It's only a matter of time."

17 YEARS, 1 MONTH, 9 HOURS, and 1 MINUTE to SILEO TERRA

April 28, 2053, 2:59 pm...

Mama's words always bounced around in my head. I wished I could do great things, but I was too busy trying to survive.

As I walked down familiar streets, I picked my next target. The house was quite small, and it appeared as though no one was around. I approached the door and quietly jiggled the knob. It was locked. Peeking in the window, I saw the interior was simple, with old, ragged, worn furniture and little else. There was also only a handful of food on the table. Straightening, I walked away. I couldn't steal their food; they didn't even have enough for themselves.

I continued walking until I arrived at the small marketplace at the end of the road. Markets were the best place to steal food. If I had enough patience, there would always be a reward.

I wandered around until I saw a fruit seller turn his back to me to talk to a customer, then grabbed the closest apple and dodged behind a crowd of people, carrying my prize.

I was just about to take a big bite when I noticed a tiny girl sitting in the dirt. She stared at me and I heard her stomach growl. We looked at each other for a few seconds without blinking. Sighing, I handed her the apple. I could always get more. As a teenager, I felt ancient, and I remembered well how it felt to be hungry and helpless at her age. Immediately, she snatched it from my hand, jumped up, and ran away.

As she passed by two men, one held out a hand to get her attention and offered her a coin with the other. Her eyes widened and she grabbed it with a shy smile. The two men looked familiar; I was sure I had seen them before. One had light skin, which was unusual. They glanced over at me and walked my way.

"Do I know you?" I asked suspiciously. I got ready to run.

The two consulted each other and the darker-skinned man answered, "We bumped into you a while ago, last year actually, but you may not remember. It was very brief." I couldn't quite place them in my memories.

"Where are your parents?"

"Gone," I replied. I thought back to the day I'd lost Mama.

⇛ 19 YEARS, 6 MONTHS, 14 DAYS, 1 HOUR, and 55 MINUTES to SILEO TERRA

November 13, 2050, 10:05 pm...

"**M**ama, you're going to be okay, right?" I held Mama's hand and saw fear in her eyes. The sickness had been slowly stealing her from me.

"I'm afraid I don't know." She sat up and stroked my head. Her voice was weak. "You have to promise me...that you'll look after yourself."

I wiped the tears from my own eyes and answered, "Mama, you know I will."

"My boy, promise me you'll make wise choices." She lay back down on the ground and pulled some rags on top of her.

"I will, Mama, but I need you. I'll be all alone." My nose was running, and my face felt hot as I buried myself in her embrace. I'd lost Baba only a year before.

"I have to go soon, Love."

"But, why?" I stared into her eyes, willing her to stay awake. I loved her more than anything.

"I don't know why...sometimes...I don't know the answer." She smiled weakly and pulled me closer.

"Mama?"

"I love you," she whispered.

"I love you too, Mama."

She closed her eyes. I pretended she was just sleeping.

⇛17 YEARS, 1 MONTH, 8 HOURS, and 43 MINUTES to SILEO TERRA

April 28, 2053, 3:17 pm...

The white man somehow understood me. He looked at me with pity in his eyes.

"I'm sorry for your loss." His friend spoke for him; his face mirrored my sadness, and I could see my pain in his eyes.

"Do you have a name, young man?" he questioned.

I hesitated, but finally I simply answered, "Alex."

"My name is Mallick, Rob Mallick. My partner here is William Derecho. We're looking for someone. Maybe you could help us..."

Suddenly gunshots rattled in my ears, cutting off our conversation. Fear coursed through my veins, but I wasn't shocked; these kinds of things happened here. Poverty bred desperation, desperation begat anger, and in my world, anger always gave birth to violence. It was common knowledge that fleeing was always the best option.

Rob's large, round eyes widened as he shouted, "We need to go!"

He grabbed my arm, but I pried it free and took a step back.

"You don't understand, Alex, we can help you. It's not safe here. We need to leave now!"

We started to run but I didn't follow them. I didn't trust them. I didn't trust anyone. They yelled my name as I sprinted away. The wind stung my face as I ran down one narrow street after another, the blur of bicycles, bricks, and crowds of people trying to escape all merging together. My only consolation was that the chilling screams and repetitive gunfire sounded further away.

"The safest place to be is up above, in the sky, looking down on your enemies." Baba had said that once.

I looked around for the highest spot I could get to...a thatched roof was my only option. Clambering up the building, I quickly gathered loose straw to cover my body. My heart throbbed in my ears, getting louder with each passing second. I held my breath; I had never been this scared.

All of a sudden, the sky fell away and the ground rose. My body slammed into the ground; the pain was unbearable. This was the end.

"I'm sorry, Baba. I'm sorry, Mama."

I couldn't do it. I hadn't had the chance to make them proud. I couldn't even keep myself alive. Then, everything faded and turned black, but just before it did, I heard, "Alex, you're going to be okay. We've got you. It's okay. Don't worry, we've got you."

"Alex, wake up! You're having a nightmare!"

I opened my eyes. Leaning my head back, I groaned, "Where am I?"

"Alex, it's okay. It's me, Rob. Remember?"

I thought for a bit, then nodded my head and looked around to get my bearings. I was lying on a bed in an empty, sterile room. A sleepy and dishevelled William peeked in to check on me. Once he saw Rob was already with me, he left us alone.

I looked down at my legs. They were different now. Metal was attached to my knees like a brace all the way down to my ankles to help me walk, and the fingers on my left hand had also been reinforced. The robotic braces on my legs weren't implanted like the metal melded into my hand, so the pain was more bearable in my aching knees than in my throbbing fingers.

A lot had changed in the last couple weeks. William and Rob had found me after the roof I had climbed up on had collapsed. They had made a split-second decision to follow me after I ran away from them. When they had reached me, I had been drifting in and out of consciousness, my legs had been severely injured, and one of my hands had been crushed beyond recognition by falling debris, yet William had been determined to save my life. They even went through the trouble of flying my broken body across the ocean to this facility, where they fixed me up and gave me a new home. This was the largest building I had ever been in.

One question had burned in the back of my mind throughout the two weeks I'd been here recovering from my near-fatal fall, and on this early morning, I finally found the courage to ask, "Rob, why did you save me?"

Rob's glasses crept down his nose as he pulled up a chair beside my bed. He plopped down and readjusted his glasses. "William and I were just about to ask you if you wanted a job working for us, kind of an assistant of sorts."

"You guys felt sorry for me."

There was more to the story than what Rob was telling me. I was sure they didn't rescue every poor kid who needed help. Or attach millions of dollars of robotic parts to them.

Rob ignored me and continued, "You'll have to learn English of course, and you'll have to spend the next few years catching up on your education."

I didn't see any other choice but to agree; I had absolutely nothing to go back to. In the end, I guess it didn't really matter why they'd chosen to help me. I sat up on my bed and rose to my feet. I was still wobbly, but I was sure I would get the hang of it soon. Slowly and hesitantly, I hobbled around the room. I gasped from the sudden pains shooting up my legs and realized perhaps my recovery would take longer than I'd thought.

"I don't know how much help I'll be," I muttered.

Rob grinned and said, "I'm sure we'll figure something out. William happens to be a genius, you know."

Walking around had drained all my energy, so I lay back down on my bed and closed my eyes. The pounding in my head had begun again. I pulled the blankets all the way up to my neck. I needed to sleep.

Things were going to be so different now, Mama and Baba.

12 YEARS, 8 MONTHS, 17 DAYS, 18 HOURS, and 1 MINUTE to SILEO TERRA

September 10, 2057, 5:59 am...

I put a glass of water down beside William. "Is there anything else I can do?" I asked. I had thought it would be a good idea to visit William before his big meeting in a couple hours. If he got the funding he was going to ask for, he would be a busy man in the months ahead. Even now, he was so busy that I spent a lot more time with Rob than William when I wasn't studying with my tutors.

He looked up at me from his desk, which displayed an elaborate multiple monitor set up. Then he looked around at the cluttered mess of papers surrounding him. Smiling, he responded, "Not at the moment. How are your legs and fingers?" He had asked me this every day for the past four years.

I looked down at the metal supporting my legs; William had upgraded the design several times. I raised my left hand so he could see it. One at a time, I moved each finger up and down. "Good."

"And how are your studies?"

I stared at him with a straight face and spoke in perfect English, "I'm almost as smart as you."

William chuckled, but then his look of amusement diminished. He stared off into the distance, resting his chin on his fist. "Oh, can you bring me a screwdriver?" He gestured to the back shelf above the office's sole window.

I walked toward the shelf and looked around for a stool. The nearby table was good enough. I jumped up on it with ease, and with one foot on the windowsill and the other planted on the tabletop, I reached for the screwdriver. I grabbed it and jumped down, spinning it around my fingers. William smiled as he watched me. I walked back to hand him the tool.

"Alex, would you give your life to save others?"

"Yes."

Nodding slowly, William continued, "Alex, you are extraordinary. You are clever and kind and self-sacrificing. I'm so glad I met you." William patted me on the shoulder and tousled my dark hair so wisps of it poked me in the eyes.

He reached his hand into his jacket pocket, hesitated, then took something out. Then he shook his head and said, "I trust you, Alex, so I'm going to show you this." For a second, I could have sworn his pale blue eyes became even more blue, as if they had brightened at the mention of a secret.

I looked down at his outstretched hand. My eyes widened and my jaw dropped. I had never seen anything like it before, but just as quickly as he had made it appear, he made it disappear, closing his hand around it and dropping it back in his pocket. "I'll tell you more later, Alex."

Mama's voice echoed in my ears. "My boy, you will do great things. It's only a matter of time."

⇛ 12 YEARS, 8 MONTHS, 15 DAYS, and 17 HOURS to SILEO TERRA

September 12, 2057, 7:00 am...

As soon as Rob entered the room, his grief was evident. "Hey, Alex, what are you doing in here?"

In the centre of William's office, surrounded by his random, sprawling algorithms scribbled across huge whiteboards, I sat on a metal stool gazing out the small window. My eyes filled with tears. William hadn't come here often since he'd worked on different projects located in different levels of the facility, but he'd always left his scribblings up to keep his mind occupied.

"Nothing," I answered dully. William was gone. Had been gone for two days. It felt like forever. Even the air felt heavy.

Rob placed his hand lightly on my shoulder.

"You rarely do nothing; I know that for a fact." He moved around me to make eye contact, but I didn't look up. Rob sighed. "You're a good kid, Alex. I'm sorry you've had to experience so much loss in your short life. I want you to know I'm going to really miss William too." A faint smile flashed over his weary face. "He made all this possible." Gesturing around him, he tried to draw my attention away from the tears collecting in his eyes.

I tried to hold back my tears, but they were too insistent. Eventually, I just let them flow down my face. Rob slowly placed a stool next to me. We sat in silence for a long time.

Then Rob whispered gently, "Alex, I was actually looking for you. I was wondering if you could help me."

I sniffled and didn't reply, but he continued anyway, "There's a reason so many of us both live and work here." I waited for him to continue but he didn't.

Finally, I guessed, "Because there's so much room?"

"Not exactly. This facility is virtually unknown to the world because the government wants us to have a secure place to work." Rob's expression was thoughtful, as if he was choosing his words carefully. He added, "You know, I think William wanted you to eventually join us."

"Join DAIR?"

Rob shook his head. "No, not just DAIR."

"What are you talking about?" I asked.

"We call ourselves DAWN: Designated Agents for the World's Needs. We are a special division within DAIR. We are inventors. We are scientists. But we are even more than that. We are protectors. We are agents."

I sat up taller in my seat, and asked, "Are you an agent?"

He nodded, "Agent Mallick, director of DAWN." He pushed his always-slipping glasses back up his nose. "I want you to join us, Alex."

I frowned and bit my lip in confusion. "You want me to become an agent?"

"Well...I mean...maybe not a field agent right away since you're still so young, but I don't think it would hurt for you to start your training. We could use someone like you. Your tutor says you're excelling in your studies even with your delayed start."

I felt my cheeks flush, but I didn't deny it.

"And you could start in the command centre, something easy."

He waited for me to respond.

"But what do you do?" I inquired curiously.

"To put it in the simplest of terms, we protect DAIR's scientific breakthroughs and inventions that aren't yet safe for public use. Ever heard of a VU?"

"No."

"Exactly. It's a vaporizing unit. I'll show you later." The corners of Rob's lips turned up slightly but then dropped again. He continued, "Of course, there are some risks to this job."

"Like what?"

"Well, it can be very dangerous. Risking your life in some cases. Letting secrets out into the world could cause absolute mayhem, so failure is not an option. But let's not get ahead of ourselves yet. You wouldn't have to worry about any of that for a long time." Rob took a deep breath and smiled. "So, are you up for it?" He clasped his hands on his lap and waited for my answer.

"Okay," I said hesitantly, "I'll do it."

"Excellent. We'll get started on your training right away, Agent..." He furrowed his brow. "Alex, I know you don't remember your last name, but you're going to have to choose one now."

"I, uh...I don't know. How do you just pick a new name? The people in my village only ever called me Boy."

"Well, I don't think Agent Boy will work," Rob replied with a grin. "You can come up with something better than that."

"How about Mallick? That sounds cool."

Rob softly chuckled and shook his head. "No, pick a different one."

≋ 12 YEARS, 8 MONTHS, 7 DAYS, 14 HOURS, and 58 MINUTES to SILEO TERRA

September 20, 2057, 9:02 am...

"This is Agent Trevor Tolli." Rob introduced me to a young man with icy blue eyes and a lopsided grin who gave me a hearty handshake.

"Hi," I said shyly.

"Agent Tolli, this is our newest member of DAWN, Agent Alex..." Rob trailed off and looked at me.

"DAWN, uh..." I stuttered nervously. I hadn't picked a last name yet.

Tolli looked confused, "Donna?"

I shook my head.

"Dona...hue?" Rob softly suggested.

"Yep, I mean, yes. That's me," I stammered awkwardly.

Tolli nodded slowly, a little confused, but he quickly replied, "Agent Donahue." Looking me up and down, he asked, "How old are you?"

I knew I was at least seventeen, maybe even eighteen, but I looked younger than that. I had joined DAWN just last week at Rob's invitation.

"Does it matter?" I challenged, already feeling embarrassed and flustered.

"No, no." Tolli shook his head, still smiling. He reminded me of a shaggy golden retriever with his full head of long, messy blonde hair.

"I'm introducing Donahue to a few DAWN agents before he starts his training. I was thinking of pairing the two of you up," Rob explained.

Just then, another guy strolled into the room, interrupting our conversation. He had spiky brown hair and cold black eyes. The bored expression on his face showed he clearly wasn't here to make friends.

"Agent Mallick, if you'll stop messing around with these *kids*, I need to speak to you."

"These *kids* are recruits, Quan, just like you were recently." Clearly annoyed, Rob led him out of the room.

Tolli pulled two chairs up to one of the tables in the small room and motioned for me to sit down. "So, I'm guessing you don't know the history behind DAWN."

"Nope."

"I've only heard some, but it's interesting. A long, long time ago" — Tolli added exaggerated hand gestures to his words — "the government discovered this guy named William Derecho, who had this incredible intellectual potential. When information about his robotics designs leaked, they persuaded him to work for them. Well, I think they basically forced him to work for them 'cause they wanted to keep a close eye on him. He also specialized in innovative modes of transportation. His first finished project was a kind of stealth aircraft with computerized windows and controls. Oh, and he also played a big part in the ongoing development of the technology that could turn hydroelectric batteries into a more sustainable form of energy. The government pretty much built DAIR up around William Derecho."

Crossing his arms and leaning back against his chair, Tolli looked up at the ceiling and nibbled his bottom lip. "Then, one day, an experiment went terribly wrong. My memory has failed me before, but I remember someone talking about the incident causing the weather to change."

"The weather? What does that have to do with anything?" I retorted.

"It created a storm out of nothing and killed some people."

"Oh." Embarrassed, I felt my cheeks grow warm.

"The government decided they needed to ramp up security to prevent more accidents from happening, but security wasn't their only concern. They needed a team that could clean up any accidental messes. DAWN was assembled to protect the secrets and the technological advancements within DAIR, pretty much at any cost."

"So, DAWN will do anything to protect these secrets?"

"Well…" He scratched his head. "Within reason, I think." Tolli paused as if he was debating whether to add more to his story.

"Is there something else?" I encouraged him to continue.

"Umm, Donahue, if you don't mind me asking…why do you have a white last name if you're not…white?" The unease on Tolli's face made me laugh nervously. I shrugged my shoulders but had a hard time controlling my laughter.

Between short breaths, I managed to get out, "It's a long story. I'll tell you sometime."

The whole thing was so ridiculous, I just started laughing harder and harder. A few tears escaped out of my eyes. Eventually, Tolli, even more confused, also started to laugh.

"Oh well…Donahue…the name suits you."

⇛ 10 YEARS, 7 MONTHS, 26 DAYS, and 33 MINUTES to SILEO TERRA

October 1, 2059, 11:27 pm...

"Your mission is to retrieve the machine and bring it to me." Rob's voice boomed from the speaker beside me. The computerized screen on the window of the cockpit projected a three-dimensional image of the machine in question.

The image showed a control box—a rectangular titanium prism—that accommodated a lever and several switches and buttons on one of the longer sides. Etched on the other side was "Whispers of Amelia." The control box had wheels attached to the bottom for quick transportation. A disc on the top was propped up horizontally by a short, thick rubber tube. This disc supported eight identical metal claws that protruded upward and curled inward like talons reaching for each other. The claws almost touched, creating a small hole in the centre that led down to the rubber tube. The hole was barely four inches in diameter while the disc was almost two feet across.

I zoomed in on the image of the control box and doubled tapped on it to see what it contained. A large liquid battery and a tangle of wires came into view.

"What the..." Tolli, my closest friend and partner since joining DAWN two years ago, leaned forward in his seat to get a closer look at the image. His focus shifted between looking at the image and piloting our two-seater aircraft.

"Cyril Elton-Blackwood created this machine. He's a tech genius who can hack into anything, and he managed to hack his way into one of DAIR's protected files and based his machine off William's old design: one that never received clearance to be built. That's what we're worried about. We have no idea what Cyril's machine can do." He paused to let the information sink in, then added, "Please stick to the plan, and don't do anything stupid..." Rob's voice trailed off.

"Are we gonna stick to the plan, Donahue?" Tolli inquired, even though he knew the answer.

I smirked as I activated the aircraft's invisibility setting with the touch of a button. "Well, that depends on whose plan." I wanted to make sure no one knew we were coming.

Rob's plan was for us to meet up with the rest of the team when we landed at our destination: a tiny, off-the-grid island in the South Seas. The team had been surveying the area for the past two days.

Our mission was to infiltrate enemy territory, more specifically, an enormous old stone building that belonged to the sinister and power-hungry Cyril. Time of contact with the rest of the team was set for 01:00 hours, but I had convinced Tolli we should land earlier in the night. We only had one chance, and I wasn't going to rely on anybody except Tolli, and possibly, our inside man on the island. The mission plan given to us had been dubious and lacking details, which had raised my suspicions about what was really going on, but Rob hadn't agreed with me.

"If we succeed and survive this mission, Agent Mallick is definitely gonna kill us." Tolli snickered at his own joke and steered the aircraft downward.

"No way," I denied, "that's not going to happen because I know what I'm doing."

"You don't even have a plan."

I responded defensively, "I have an idea."

Tolli wiped the sweat from his forehead and concluded, "Oh man, we're gonna die." This time, he didn't laugh.

The aircraft slowed as we prepared for an abrupt landing. I selected our weapons and grabbed two sets of night goggles.

As soon as we touched down, the hatch on the bottom opened, revealing the stifling darkness of the night.

"Trust me," I whispered as I leapt out.

I landed on the ground silently, and Tolli stayed close behind. We looked over at a heavily guarded, isolated building far in the distance and watched the spotlights from the high watchtowers dancing over the ground.

A rustle in the bushes startled me. Tolli and I dropped to the ground.

A dark figure walked forward from behind a cluster of trees. "We know you're here. Hands up. This is your only warning."

The slender shadow was visible through my night goggles. I watched as he pressed on his earpiece and said, "It was nothing, sir. No threat detected. It was just a raccoon. The project is safe." He removed it and walked straight toward us.

"You guys are going to get caught," he warned. His dark hair jutted from his scalp in tufts, which reminded me of a hedgehog. It was the same mohawk he'd sported every day since the first day I'd met him. I breathed a sigh of relief. It was Kyler Quan, normally my least favourite person in the world, but not today.

"We had it under control," I grumbled as I stood up. "Is your earpiece off?"

"What do you think you're doing? You were supposed to meet me at 01:00 sharp with the rest of the team. Of course, I turned it off."

"Change of plans." The lie came easily. The next bit was true. "I think there might be a mole. We didn't want to risk our one chance at getting that machine."

About six months ago, two agents had gone missing and were presumed dead. Their mission had been to get the coordinates of this island to us. They'd managed to get one last cryptic message to us before losing contact: *11.1778° N, 102.8451° W. Cover compromised. Will make contact when safe.*

Even though I couldn't see him that well, I knew Kyler was rolling his eyes. Surprisingly, he stopped questioning me and turned on his heels, gesturing for us to follow him.

Tolli said accusingly, "For the record, I blame Donahue."

I hissed at him under my breath, "Gee, thanks Tolli. Let's go."

Months earlier, Kyler had skillfully infiltrated Cyril's team, gaining their trust as head of security. I had to admit he was an excellent agent. He handed us two uniforms, and we slipped them on. Now we could blend right in with the other guards.

The wind whistled in my ears, and the grass swished around my boots as we trudged on through the night. At least entering the building was easy. We walked right in and followed Kyler up to the top floor.

"You sure no one will notice us?" I asked.

Kyler answered confidently, "No one will notice you."

"Or think we're being suspicious up here?" Tolli added.

"There are guards up here all the time."

The hairs on the back of my neck bristled. I didn't believe him for one second; something wasn't right. After walking down an empty hallway, we arrived at a giant round door guarded by two armed men. Kyler walked up to confront them. Next to the guards, he looked even scrawnier than normal.

"Code: CYR17N0W. Urgent matter. Cyril is expecting me to move the project to another location. We got wind of an upcoming attack." Surprisingly, Kyler sounded convincing.

The bald guard pulled out a small screen. Still staring down at it, he confirmed, "Access granted."

The metal door swung open. Red laser beams hummed as they protected the wall behind them. The deadly beams switched off, revealing the outline of a single door the same colour as the wall. Kyler reached out and twisted the doorknob. It opened easily.

As Kyler walked through, he puffed out his chest and whispered to us, "Nobody gets in unless they have Cyril's trust."

Annoyed, Tolli and I followed him into a vast open space, floored and walled in concrete, where our targeted machine was guarded by a semi-invisible shield that glowed a pinky purple and was deadly to the touch.

"How do we get past the shield?" I eagerly asked.

From a shadow in the corner of the room came a sinister chuckle, "You can't...and you won't."

Kyler walked away from us and joined the countless armed guards that had swarmed in after us. "You really thought you could waltz in here and grab the machine?"

Tolli's eyes burned with anger as he spat out, "Traitor!"

I thought back to when Kyler turned off his earpiece; he must have lied and kept it on. We had just allowed him to walk us right into their trap. At least the rest of the team was still out there somewhere.

"DAWN is weak; it won't survive," Kyler jeered, "Cyril knows how this world works, and he's determined to come out on top. He is the future, and I'm going to take my chances with him."

A stocky man with hair slicked back against his head stepped out from the group. Scowling at Tolli and I with his teeth bared, Cyril reminded me of a bulldog. Dark stubble covered his round jaw, and his crooked nose competed for attention against the large jagged scar on his right cheek.

Cyril's past had told us all we needed to know about his drive to innovate. We'd been briefed before we'd left on this mission. He had once been the DAWN agent overseeing the time studies division at DAIR, and he specialized in digital operations. Then his little girl got sick. Cyril was sure DAIR had technology that could cure her and had begged them to release it to him, but they had told him it wasn't ready. As a result, Amelia Elton-Blackwood, Cyril's seven-year-old daughter, had passed away. His failure to save his daughter had enraged and consumed him. He'd left DAIR and vowed revenge, diving into his work to distract himself from his grief. He became even more determined to produce better, faster results than DAIR. Cyril was now the guy who took short cuts and didn't hesitate to remove obstacles in his way.

Cocking his head to the side, he sneered, "It's only a matter of time before everything is out of your reach, out of your control. Scientific breakthroughs are happening every day, and DAIR just wants to hide everything they discover. You have the technology to help people, but you hide it. You call yourselves protectors of humanity but, really, you're just trying to protect yourselves."

"No!" Tolli protested.

"What were you going to do with my Amelia?" Cyril asked, gesturing to his machine. "Destroy it or use it? Or even worse, lock it up?"

He didn't wait for us to reply. "I know all about you, Alex and Trevor, what drives you, where you came from, where you're going. You don't know what I know. I've seen things, and it's given me a purpose I will fulfill." After a brief, thoughtful pause, he added, "You can't possibly imagine what is to come."

"And you can?" Tolli shot back quietly.

"Everyone will be so disappointed when you don't return." Stroking the pistol at his hip, Cyril laughed, "Ah, well, I guess you'll all end up in the same place soon. Hold them down!"

The guards forced us to our knees. As Cyril aimed his weapon at us, we looked up at him, straight in the eye. We might be staring death in the face, but we weren't going to be cowards about it.

A piercing shot broke Cyril's concentration, followed by another shot and another. DAWN had arrived, and with it, hope and courage flooded back into my heart like the sun bursting over the horizon and chasing away the darkness.

I craned my head around and strained to see what was going on behind me. Out of the corner of my eye, I caught a quick glimpse of a figure behind me, emerging out of the shadows. With a magnificent flurry of swift roundhouse kicks that were a sight to see, she dropped some of the guards behind me. Then the guard pinning me down on my knees was knocked to the ground. Blood gushed from his nostrils as he slumped, unconscious. I glanced up and watched her move on to fight other guards, executing punches and kicks perfectly, her chin-length dark hair swishing from side to side, matching the rhythm of her graceful movements.

Before I could thank her, she glared at me and said, "I'm Agent Viola. You guys are in big trouble."

Her aim was impeccable as she fired her laser taser, a pistol-like weapon with a strap on the handle and a red slash down its length, at a guard coming at us. He went down and she fired again. A red taser bullet bounced off the wall and into another guard's neck, paralyzing him immediately. These bullets were designed to render the target unconscious rather than kill them. That was how DAWN operated. Agent Viola continued fighting, and I watched, dumbfounded. I had never seen someone so skilled in combat.

Tolli yelled, "Hey, Vee! Good to see you again. Can I get some help here?"

I snapped out of my trance and rushed to Tolli's aid. My fist connected with the nose of one of Tolli's captors, and Tolli smashed the butt end of a stolen pistol over the other's head.

I looked over and saw Kyler on his back; one look at his body told us his neck had been broken. For a brief moment, I wondered which of my colleagues had killed him.

In the midst of the chaos, Cyril had deactivated Amelia's shield. He scurried to the machine's controls, pressing buttons and switching on dials, and then grabbed a set of silencing headphones. Dodging bullets and laser taser bullets and manoeuvring around unconscious bodies and puddles of blood, I weaved toward him, but I was too late. He had activated the machine.

Bursting through a small opening in the ceiling I hadn't noticed before, a bright light beamed out into the starry sky. An intense humming noise began to resonate in my ears, and it felt as though my eardrums were being ripped out of my head. I clamped my palms tightly against the sides of my head in a feeble attempt to drown out the noise.

"MAKE IT STOP!" I yelled, but even I couldn't hear my voice above the roar of the machine.

People started stumbling around me, losing focus on the fight in front of them as they desperately grabbed at their ears.

Summoning all my remaining strength, and the help of my robotics, I approached Cyril, hands still clasped to my ears. I had to stop him.

I feinted left and lunged to the right, connecting my elbow with his jaw. He wasn't expecting it, so after recovering from the blow, he blindly threw a few punches in an attempt to keep me away. It was obvious he wasn't a fighter. Again, sacrificing my ears, I threw a punch to his head with my left hand. My metal fist hit him spot on.

His grip released and the machine gradually stopped, along with the whining and whirring. Sluggishly, Cyril slumped to the ground. I had reopened his scar.

The DAWN agents regrouped and created a tight formation around Agent Viola, who wheeled Amelia toward the nearest exit. Tolli and I dragged Cyril behind them, and, as fast as we could, we made our way outside.

The cool night breeze met us as we walked out the doors, and we took turns carrying Cyril until we got to the larger aircraft that had carried the other agents. When Tolli and I were sure he was contained and heading back to headquarters, we sprinted back to our own aircraft.

It was 02:00 hours when we departed the island.

Cyril would have to face justice, and I would have to face Rob.

⇛ 10 YEARS, 7 MONTHS, 24 DAYS, 16 HOURS, and 49 MINUTES to SILEO TERRA

October 3, 2059, 7:11 am...

Rob sat in front of me with his hands folded tightly on his standard beige metal desk. I could feel the tension emanating from him, see it in the lines on his forehead, and hear it in his voice as he lectured me.

"But at least it's not the end of the world. Yesterday's mission was still a success. Tolli and I delivered the machine and Cyril to you, and we exposed Kyler."

Solemnly, Rob nodded. "Donahue, that machine is extremely dangerous." His voice escalated as he struggled to control his emotions. "And you should have waited for the rest of the agents! You almost died!"

I refused to apologize. We stared at each other for a long minute.

Finally, Rob yielded and sighed. He turned his computer screen to show me the diagnostics of Cyril's machine. "Using a liquid battery powered by a mixture of chemicals and an intense jolt of electricity, it can home in on a specific coordinate in another dimension. The strong pull of the machine causes a portal-like hole to open in that dimension. With access to that dimension, which contains the threads of time, we could potentially control time itself. With enough time and research, we could even have the ability to foresee future events."

"That sounds dangerous."

"Well, we wouldn't use it until we knew what we were dealing with...but...if something catastrophic happens and we need to undo something, that could possibly be a last resort."

I held my tongue. I wasn't the one in charge. Even so, my mind raced with the possible consequences of playing with time.

Rob sighed loudly, breaking my train of thought. "I've been putting this off for a while, but you should know William Derecho has a relative in this complex."

I looked up at him in shock. "Seriously?"

"Yes, a niece. She's just like you, um…sort of. There have been some…difficulties. Maybe it's time you meet her. She needs a distraction from her…project. Ever since William's death, she's been having a very difficult time."

I stood, speechless.

"William had wanted to introduce you to her…but…but then…the accident happened." He kept pausing as if every word hurt.

"Why wouldn't you tell me?" I questioned. Was there actually someone like me?

"I didn't know what would happen, how she would react. I didn't want to put extra stress on her." He ran his fingers through his short, thick hair. "She didn't want to talk to anyone; even now she doesn't want anything to do with the outside world. She was severely traumatized, and her temper—"

"How long has she been here?!" I exclaimed.

Rob's gaze dropped to the floor. "It's been around…oh, eight years. She had nowhere else to go."

I rubbed my palms on my eyes. I didn't know how to respond to that.

"Donahue, you don't understand. She's not like you—I mean she is but she's—"

"She's what?!" I demanded.

Rob sighed, "She's strong. She's fast. She's intelligent. But she's also very angry. And she can't control it."

"So, you keep her locked up? Like a prisoner?" I blurted.

"Donahue, she doesn't want to leave." Rob opened his mouth to continue but I stood up and turned to the door. Thrusting my hands up in disbelief, I walked out of the room.

Rob's voice barely reached me in my fury. "Room T-117!"

After a quick detour to grab some breakfast, I found myself in front of the room number Rob had given me. I knocked on the door, but no one answered. "Hello?"

"Wait," a voice commanded.

I heard a few clinks and the sound of a key being pulled out.

I slowly turned the doorknob to peek in. A girl was lying on the ground, her back facing me. A small pistol-like device with a string attached to it sat on the ground beside her. At the end of the string was the door's key.

She mumbled more to herself than to me, "I press the button and it retracts the string, pulling the key out so I don't have to get up. Genius."

Her skin was ghostly pale, and her fiery red hair was splayed out on the floor around her. Slowly, she sat up to face me. At first glance, she appeared weak and thin until you noticed her robotic parts. Dark circles outlined her emerald green eyes, and for a second, I thought I saw blue rings around her irises. I blinked and they were gone. Without breaking my gaze, she rose and walked toward me.

"You're not Rob. What do you want?" The girl drew closer.

I put my hands up in defence. "I just want to talk."

Her eyes found the metal that supported my legs. I almost always wore shorts when I wasn't working; they were so much easier to manoeuvre around my knees. She froze, but only for a moment. "What's your name?"

"Alex Donahue."

She seemed to recognize my name, which surprised me. She reached out and grabbed my hand and shook it. Her gaze fell to the metal on my fingers.

"Alex, you knew my uncle. I'm Wren Derecho, his niece."

I nodded. To make her feel more at ease, I pulled a wooden chair toward me and plopped down. "I was..." I searched for the right words, "close to your uncle."

She nodded, also taking a seat. "He was..."

"Brilliant and kind of crazy but also one of my closest friends," I finished.

"Alex, you sort of remind me of him." Wearily, she grinned, "Not in your appearance, of course, but there's something else…" She stared at me for a few moments before changing the subject. "Has anyone ever called you Donna?"

"No, and don't you start." I wrinkled my nose in distaste.

"Why? Donna's got a nice ring to it," Wren mocked.

I must have looked annoyed because she started to laugh, "You know, Donna, I'd like to show you my current project. That's why you came, right?"

She didn't wait for a reply but instead strolled across the room toward something under a tarp.

"This is Tempus II," she said as she yanked off the plastic.

I stared in disbelief at the pyramid-like machine. It had a large, thin rod situated on top of it, round windows, and one seat inside. Why was everyone obsessed with time?

All that escaped my mouth was, "You can't."

"But I can." Just like that, she slipped back into a dark mood.

This whole thing seemed wrong to me. She was interfering with things that were not supposed to be messed with. Time shouldn't be manipulated by anyone, not by DAIR, not by DAWN, not by crazy hackers, and not even by this innocent emerald-eyed girl.

⇛ 9 YEARS, 7 MONTHS, 8 DAYS, 11 HOURS, and 50 MINUTES to SILEO TERRA

October 19, 2060, 12:10 pm...

Wren kicked the pistol out of my hand and dove to retrieve it. Rolling onto her back, she placed her finger on the trigger, aiming it at my heart.

"Hey, stop—"

She shifted and pulled the trigger, the target behind me lighting up to indicate she had hit it.

I shook my head. "You shouldn't shoot that thing so close to me. You're supposed to treat it like a real gun. Besides, we're on the same side!"

She laughed lightheartedly. We were training in an underground room in the facility. The targets were holograms of dark figures that moved around in a maze of moving walls about five feet tall. This particular room included a weapons rack, a boxing arena, an obstacle course, and a maze used for target practice.

"Okay, I think we're done for today." It seemed like a good time to finish.

Wren stood up and lightly shoved me, experimenting with her strength. Losing my footing, I toppled over and crashed into the wall. That was going to leave a bruise. I laughed despite the pain.

Wren looked surprised. "You okay, Donna?" Wren asked apologetically as she helped me up. "Sorry, you know I'm still figuring out my own strength."

"Yeah, you can really do some damage," I replied, massaging my shoulder.

We grabbed our bags and walked down one of the bare hallways of the complex.

She recalled a time just after we had met, about a year ago. "Remember when Tolli first saw us walking together?"

Tolli had stopped dead in his tracks. He had just assumed I was the only one with robotics. Then Tolli had said he had no idea I had a girlfriend, and Wren and I had laughed hard. It was kind of funny then but not as much now. I cared deeply for her; I just didn't know how to tell her.

As if on cue, Tolli sprinted up to me. His face was flushed, and he was out of breath, but he managed to gasp, "Donahue! We have a serious situation!"

Just then, the security alarm went off, causing my senses to heighten and my heart to beat faster.

"What did you do?" I demanded, half-jokingly.

"Not me. Cyril escaped."

"What? How?!" I yelled.

"How in the world am I supposed to know?" he yelled back, tossing me a laser taser. "What are you waiting for? Let's go!"

We broke into a sprint. Glancing back, I noticed Wren at my heels. She dashed past Tolli and me and took the lead. Even when she nearly tripped over her own feet, Wren was unquestionably the fastest person I had ever met. Even though Rob's suggestion that I help train her in combat was more to distract her from her obsession over completing Tempus II, I could see Wren becoming a huge asset for DAWN in the future. When I had suggested it to Rob, he had said he wanted the best for Wren. I wasn't sure if he'd meant the best for Wren was not to be a part of DAWN so I didn't push it. In any case, I didn't think it would hurt to help her be physically and mentally ready if the time came. I could already see that the mental readiness would be the more difficult of the two. I rubbed my shoulder as I ran after her.

Suddenly Wren screeched to a halt, and Tolli and I had to make some quick adjustments midstride to avoid running into her. Cyril stood in the hallway with two heavily armed DAWN agents protecting him. Blood stained Cyril's forehead.

He narrowed his eyes when he saw Tolli and I. "So, we meet again. My arch nemesis-es…er, nemesi? Whatever."

Cyril shifted his pistol to Wren. "Now, let us through or I'll kill your girlfriend."

"Why does everyone think that?" I blurted.

Wren cut me off before I could say anything else. "You think you could actually kill me?"

Cyril replied, clearly exasperated, "I don't have time for this." He pulled the trigger.

She didn't even flinch when the pistol went off. She just put her hand up and then slowly lowered it, opening her palm to reveal the bullet.

We all stared at it in disbelief.

Cyril was contained in an electric force field that glowed a soft magenta. Even though I had advised Wren against it—spending hours trying to reason with her—she had insisted on joining me when I went to question Cyril.

Cyril glared at us when he saw us enter. "Hmmm, looks like they found another broken human to experiment on."

Wren's expression was grave. She raised her metal hand and picked at her lower lip, furrowing her brows. Was she flustered? I thought maybe disturbed was a better word. I breathed slowly, trying to remain calm, hoping Wren could control her temper. I wanted to know more about how Cyril had escaped, and that meant I needed to get him to talk. Cautiously, I walked closer.

Wren gritted her teeth but followed close behind me. Absentmindedly, she fished the luminescent orb out of her pocket and rolled it around her fingers.

The orb's reflection immediately caught Cyril's eye. Squinting at her hand, Cyril lowered his voice, "I know you. You're a threat to everyone in this building. What's keeping you from killing everyone?"

"Would you like to be first?" Wren threatened, jamming the orb back into its hiding place.

"If it's not me, it'll be someone else. It's your fate. Yet if someone can control time, they can also control fate. Who wouldn't want that?" Cyril paused, then calmly added, "I know what loss can do to a person. They would sacrifice anything for a second chance. But the timeline is changing now. I've seen things you couldn't comprehend. Trust me, I know."

"I don't trust you at all," I said. "You sound like a lunatic."

He closed his eyes for a moment and then reopened them, focusing his gaze again on Wren. "You wouldn't kill me. If you did, you'd prove me right."

Wren narrowed her eyes. "About what?"

Cyril leaned forward and hissed, "You wield a weapon no person can control. I can see you're already a slave to its power. If you kill me, you'd be the corrupted one. William Derecho was a complete fool messing with that stuff!" He spat.

Wren winced at the mention of her uncle.

"So was your dad," Cyril added, pushing the dagger deeper.

Wren broke.

The orb sparked in response. Blue sparks leapt into Wren's skin and buried themselves in her eyes with the same brilliant blue replacing the emerald flecks.

"Wren?" I gulped.

Her voice was as cold as ice. "Get out of my way."

I stepped between her and Cyril, but Wren reached out to push me aside. The orb bled through her touch and the sparks turned on me, pulsing with unrestrained energy.

Then a sheet of darkness descended on me.

9 YEARS, 6 MONTHS, 15 DAYS, 10 HOURS, and 55 MINUTES to SILEO TERRA

November 12, 2060, 1:05 pm...

Everything was blurry when I opened my eyes. I lifted my head slightly.

"What in the world happened?" My voice was hoarse.

Vee looked up from her book and jumped up in surprise. It took her a few seconds to find her voice, "Donahue! The doctors were sure you weren't going to wake up! Ever! You've been in a coma for nearly a month!"

"Hey, Vee," I croaked. "Well, I showed them, didn't I?"

"You sure did...um..." She paused, far away for a second, before shaking her head and continuing. "Sorry, Wren is kind of going crazy..." She walked over to me. "Are you okay?" she asked gently. Despite the churning in my stomach and the dizzy feeling in my head, I managed to nod. Vee unlocked the wheels of my hospital bed. " I'm going to get in so much trouble for this, and I hate to stress you out, but you need to see Wren right away. We'll get the doctor after. Grab your IV pole."

Vee rolled me toward the door and caught me up on what had been happening as we slowly made our way through the hallways to Wren's room. When we arrived, she knocked on the door.

"Wren? Wren, I have some good news."

A faint red flash from underneath the door interrupted her. Vee's face paled as she tried to turn the doorknob.

"What's the matter, Vee?" I demanded.

Vee began to tremble. She whispered, "These past few weeks have been torture for her. She hasn't said a word to anyone except me."

Desperately, she beat her fists against the metal door. "Wren! Open up! It's me!" She looked at me. "Help me, Donahue!" she yelled frantically.

I knew banging on the door would do nothing. "Hairpin."

She plucked one out of her short, messy ponytail and tossed it to me. "Push me up to the door."

As I started to pick the lock, Vee mumbled, "Wren said this was all too much. She couldn't handle the thought of losing you."

Another blinding flash, this one bright red, flickered beneath the door. I locked my eyes with Vee's. That distinctive red flash told us all we needed to know.

"Was that a memory eraser? How did she get her hands on one?!" The words tumbled out of me. "She'll delete us all." I didn't feel the weight of the words until they fell out of my mouth. I could barely breathe.

Finally, the door unlocked and swung open. Wren stood in the middle of the room staring blankly at us. Vee slowly walked toward her.

Suspiciously, Wren squinted at us and asked, "Who are you?"

A white, cylinder-shaped object speckled with silver fell out of her hand, pulsing red. The memory eraser was small, but the damage it did was great. She placed a hand on her forehead and winced in pain. "What happened?"

9 YEARS, 6 MONTHS, 11 DAYS, 23 HOURS, and 43 MINUTES to SILEO TERRA

November 16, 2060, 12:17 pm...

I rolled myself outside in my wheelchair to get some fresh air. I was still recuperating from the coma, so the doctors had recommended I still use it to get around. Raindrops began to fall around me, but I didn't want to go back inside. The clouds were so dark, it seemed like night had fallen mid-day.

Rob had sent Tolli and Vee off that morning to get more help for Wren from a specialist. They needed to bring in someone who knew about the technology used in the memory eraser, more specifically, the neurological damage it could cause. When activated, the machine connected to the electrical activity inside the brain and fried neurons associated with the memory you wanted to erase. Wren had tried to delete too much. The doctors were doing whatever they could, making sure Wren was physically stable—helping her become mentally stable would come later—and putting her through numerous tests and scans to try and assess what areas of her brain the memory eraser had affected.

The rain drenched my clothes and I remembered a song Mama used to sing to me.

"The sky is weeping..."

I jumped in my seat as the sound of a thunderclap boomed right above the roof of the large facility behind me. My ears started ringing and I covered them instinctively.

"Lightning is leaping..."

I turned around to see an enormous bolt of lightning turn from bright white to a blazing blue. But the weird part was that it didn't let up.

"The sun has said goodnight…"

A flash of blue filled the entire inside of the building, shattering all the windows.

"The darkness of night…"

Thunder shook the ground I sat on.

"Says it's time to sleep…"

What kind of storm was this?

"My boy, lay your head to rest."

And then there was only silence.

Suddenly, a small figure burst through the front door without opening it, reducing it to splinters and leaving a massive hole in the walls around it. Lightning crackled from her body. It was Wren, and even from a distance, I could see her eyes were shining the same blue as the orb. I stood up to go help her but froze when I realized the lightning wasn't hurting her. It was following her; she was manipulating it. The colour drained from my face.

I watched in shock as she turned and walked away from me, and Cyril's words resounded in my head and sent a chill down my spine, "You wield a weapon no person can control. I can see you're already a slave to its power."

PART THREE
CASSANDRA VIOLA

⋙ 19 YEARS, 5 MONTHS, 17 DAYS, 13 HOURS, and 59 MINUTES to SILEO TERRA

December 10, 2050, 10:01 am...

I was going on an adventure.

My mom and I were finally moving to our new house in Ashborne. My dad had already been working and living there for about two months, but Mom had had to stay behind to finalize the sale of our old house and arrange for our belongings to be packed and moved. We were all going to be together again, and I was so excited.

As we pulled up to our new house, I couldn't sit still from the excitement growing in my chest. The outside of the house was nothing special to look at with its dark gray siding and stone steps, but there were a few things inside I couldn't wait to see. Mom had told me about the walk-in closet in my new room, the hot tub on the back porch, and the best part—a skylight in the living room.

I opened the door of our compact car and was greeted by a cold, icy wind that stung my face. I looked down the snow-covered street and saw a tiny red-haired girl staring at me from her front porch on the opposite side of the street just a few doors down. I looked to make sure there were no cars coming and slowly made my way toward her.

"Cassandra, where are you going?" Mom called out after me.

"I just want to say hi to that girl." I pointed across the street, and my mom's nod and smile gave me the go ahead.

The girl hesitated at first, staying where she was, but eventually, she began to walk to meet me. As she neared the end of her driveway, she slipped, awkwardly losing her balance and crashing onto the icy concrete.

"Are you okay?!" I shouted, concerned. I slid over to her and braced myself so I could help her to her feet without falling myself.

She brushed off the snow and dirt from her knees and replied with a grin, "Yup, I'm fine. My name's Wren. What's yours?"

"Cassandra."

"That's too long. I'm just going to call you Cass."

And that was how our friendship began.

⇛ 18 YEARS, 5 MONTHS, 3 DAYS, 9 HOURS, and 13 MINUTES to SILEO TERRA

December 24, 2051, 2:47 pm...

It was Christmas Eve. The doorbell rang, and I rushed to open it. Wren stood in the doorway, and her bright green eyes were filled with excitement as she gestured for me to come outside to play in the freshly fallen snow. I reached for a fleece toque and my mom's old winter jacket and squirmed into puffy pink snow pants. I had known Wren for a year now, and we had become best friends. Once I'd gotten to know her, she hadn't been shy around me anymore.

As I slipped on my well-worn mittens, I yelled out, "Are you excited for Christmas?"

"Of course I am, Cass! I'm hoping for a hoodie that's not too big." To make her point, she flapped her arms and jumped around until her long sleeves escaped way past the cuffs of her jacket.

I wiggled my hand, showing her the hole my pinky finger had made. "I need new mittens," I giggled.

Wren pulled a fuzzy purple ball out of her coat pocket and handed it to me. Mittens! They had two tiny blackbirds on them. I thanked her as I slipped them on.

"No problem," she replied with a smile.

We spent hours building a snow fort and tall menacing snowmen to guard it; the snow was the perfect texture, making a crunching sound as we pushed it all around us. When we got tired and wanted a break, we lay on our backs to look up at the sky and make angels in the snow. I could spend all my free time with Wren and still never get tired of her.

My house had a skylight in the living room, and my favourite time to look through it was at night. If you focused on the dark sky, it felt like you were in space.

I had invited Wren over for a sleepover, and the clear, starry sky was perfect. We stared up at the bright lights.

"Hey, Cass, I saw a shooting star!" Wren whispered from beneath her blankets.

We were supposed to be asleep, so we had to talk in whispers.

"Make a wish!" I urged. I silently wished we could be friends forever even though I wasn't the one who'd seen the shooting star.

Wren closed her eyes and took a second to think. "I wish…"

I looked over at her, but she had fallen asleep mid-sentence. I giggled and pulled her blankets up around her shoulders. Maybe my wish would come true after all. My fingers got caught in Wren's red bird's nest of hair. I smiled, a deep affection suddenly blooming inside me. I was never going to let anything bad happen to her.

I whispered, "I promise I will always be here for you, Wren. No matter what."

The moon was now clearly visible, and it was shining so brightly, I didn't think I would ever fall asleep. Space seemed to be at my fingertips, and the stars welcomed me with their twinkly winks. I didn't remember closing my eyes, but the next thing I knew, I was floating—floating through space.

18 YEARS, 2 MONTHS, 11 DAYS, 2 HOURS, and 30 MINUTES to SILEO TERRA

March 16, 2052, 9:30 pm...

I squatted at the top of the stairs, holding my breath and trying not to be seen. My parents were arguing downstairs again, something that seemed to be happening a lot more lately.

"You don't even care!"

"I'm trying to help you, Angela!"

"You're not even here!"

"What do you want me to do?!"

They always waited until they thought I was asleep, but how could anyone sleep with all the noise they made? The yelling and fighting and crying only stopped when my dad went away on business. Maybe that was just the way things had to be in our family.

I slowly let my breath out and carefully crawled back to my room, slipping into my cozy bed. I stared up at the glowing stars I had taped on the ceiling. Why did people fight? What good did it do? And why did it hurt me when I wasn't even the one fighting? It all seemed pretty pointless to me.

My eyes glazed over with sudden tears. I had to force myself to think of something else.

Wren had gone out of town today to go visit her uncle, and I missed her already. Hopefully, I could finish my homework by tomorrow afternoon so I could go over to her place.

A knock on the front door startled me. My parents stopped yelling.

After a slight pause, I heard voices at the door but couldn't make out what they were saying. Curiosity got the best of me, and I crept back over to my place at the top of the stairs overlooking the front door.

Two people stood just inside the door. One was an extremely tall man with square glasses that matched his square face. The other was a woman, her dirty blonde hair pulled back into a tight bun. They were both wearing matching dark uniforms. As she turned to look around the room, I read the word "POLICE" on the back of her uniform.

"I'm really sorry," she apologized.

"When did it happen?" Mom whispered.

"About six hours ago. All we know is that it was a really bad accident, but no other cars were involved."

"How do we tell Cass, Mark?" Her voice quivered.

Dad didn't answer.

I emerged from the shadows. "Tell me what?" I inquired suspiciously.

The four adults stared up at me. Finally, the male police officer broke the silence and said gently, "Cassandra, your friend Wren and her parents were in a car accident today. It's not good."

12 YEARS, 27 DAYS, 14 HOURS, and 14 MINUTES to SILEO TERRA

April 30, 2058, 9:46 am...

The signs in the gym window caught my attention as I wandered aimlessly along Main Street in downtown Ashborne. Advertisements for different MMA classes caught my attention, so I stopped to examine them.

I was in desperate need of a distraction. My parents had divorced four years ago, two years after Wren's accident, and I had felt completely lost ever since. It suddenly dawned on me that my habit of aimlessly wandering the streets reflected how I had been mindlessly making my way through life.

I pushed the door open and crinkled my nose at the smell of stale sweat that wafted out. I walked in and picked up one of the sign-up sheets from the front desk. A quick glance through the information told me I would be old enough to join when I turned eighteen next month.

"Hey! I'm Silvia Mercier. Are you interested in MMA?" I glanced up to see a woman with white shoulder-length hair. She looked too young to have white hair, but it suited her well, ironically lending to the cool, trendy vibe she gave off.

She gestured to the sheet in my hands. "It's a great way to work out and really fun to learn."

I looked back at the sheet. "I don't know. I'll have to think about it. Do you work here?"

Silvia laughed, "No, I just train here. Sorry if I seem pushy. It's just nice to see a new face around here, especially a girl."

Someone called her name from the far side of the gym, and she turned and gave them a nod. Before she turned to leave, she gave me a warm smile and whispered, "Think about it."

As I headed back out the door, I took a deep breath of fresh air. Maybe this was what I needed. Who knows? Maybe I would even like it.

11 YEARS, 4 MONTHS, 26 DAYS, and 15 HOURS to SILEO TERRA

January 1, 2059, 9:00 am...

I walked into the gym and grabbed a pair of grappling gloves without slowing my pace. I headed straight over to the punching bag to warm up. There were a few other people there already, so I had to wait before I could get started. Once I did, Silvia strode over and took her usual spot beside me. I had joined the MMA gym six months ago, and Silvia had taken me under her wing. She was athletic and passionate about working out, and truthfully, she was just a nice person to be around. Silvia provided a reprieve to all the drama in my life with her positive, cheerful demeanour. Perhaps it was because she had never bothered to get married that she was so carefree.

I kept my fist clenched tightly and threw a punch at the bag, making sure to rotate in one swift motion.

Silvia commented, "Do it again, but harder! Good. Again! Keep your guard up. Harder!"

Sweat began to appear on my forehead.

"This..." I exhaled as I threw punch after punch, "is...for...leaving... my...mother."

I took a deep breath in. I was learning to control my anger, but once in a while, it felt so good let it out. Silvia looked at me with concern but didn't say anything.

I stepped back and kicked the bag repeatedly. After a few more roundhouse kicks, I felt a little better.

Silvia beckoned to me to put on my protective gear. I slipped my headgear on and stepped into the boxing ring.

Silvia tied back her white hair into a tight ponytail. "Your elbow is one of the hardest parts of your body. Use it. Be light on your feet and keep your hands up."

She ran through her list of advice every time we sparred. When she was finished her spiel, she positioned herself with her fists up, a little bounce in her step.

I blocked her first punch and answered with a kick to her knee. Silvia threw an uppercut to my jaw and jabbed her elbow into my chest. I jumped back to dodge her next punch. She returned to her fighting stance with her fists tucked under her chin, and I mirrored her.

When she went for another strike, I crouched under her outstretched arm and slipped behind her. I kicked the back of her knees and dug my elbow into her back. She stumbled forward.

She panted, "You're getting good, Cass."

I smiled and turned to grab my water bottle. After taking several big gulps of water, I wiped the sweat from my brow.

Silvia's eyes never left me, and she waited until both of us had caught our breath. "If you don't mind me asking, why do you like MMA?"

I took a moment to think about her question and then replied, my chest still heaving, "I like being able to release some of my anger."

"You have a rare talent I haven't seen in a long time…maybe ever. Have you ever thought of putting your skills to use for the good of others? Perhaps even for the good of the world?" She had a determined look in her eyes as she took off her grappling gloves. "You could protect others, help others, and give your life a purpose?"

I thought of Wren. I trusted and respected Silvia more than anyone else in this world. Normally, I would have ended a conversation like this by walking away, but I felt safe with Silvia, so I decided to answer her. "Silvia, I had a friend who died in a car accident. I had no control over it. If I could have protected her…"

"I'm so sorry, Cass."

A moment of silence passed. Then Silvia changed the subject, "If you're really passionate about fighting, then keep up the good work, and

I'll recommend you to a special training facility where you could learn to protect others. You could work with others who want to help make the world just a little bit better."

"Oh?" She had piqued my interest.

"At the end of the month, they're accepting new applicants—but only with a recommendation."

"Applicants?" I questioned curiously.

Silvia grinned. "My employer, DAWN."

⇛ 11 YEARS, 3 MONTHS, 18 HOURS, and 2 MINUTES to SILEO TERRA

February 28, 2059, 5:58 am...

"You've been training hard in hopes of joining DAWN: Designated Agents for the World's Needs. Now let me remind you that only a handful of you will make it to the end," Agent Quan told us yet again. He stood on a chair so he could see above the other initiates. His mohawk made him look taller than he actually was.

During this past month of training, I had excelled in every area. I had been initially drawn to MMA because it offered me a release from my anger, but now I could see my combat skills could be used for something far greater than myself. I could protect others. That idea had become the most compelling motivational factor to push myself to improve. I could do for others what I couldn't do for Wren. The training had also helped me control my anger by giving me a feeling of peace and icy calmness that had enabled me to reach a skill level far beyond the other initiates and that had exceeded my trainers' expectations.

Silvia spoke, her voice jolting me out of my thoughts, "I'd like to congratulate all of you for making it this far. Your training is almost complete. All that remain are two tests. This initial test will be like nothing you have ever experienced before. It consists of a simulated mission that will force you to draw from your training and will expose any weaknesses. There will be four teams of three, and each team will have a different mission. You won't be issued any weapons, so if you want them, you'll have to figure out how to acquire them. The ones used in this exercise are called ghost blasters, and they rely on a laser system, not dissimilar to a toy laser gun, but with the characteristics of a high-calibre rifle. If you're hit, the laser will immediately cause temporary paralysis, and the sensors on your shoulders will flash, indicating you are eliminated. Remain calm. Someone will come to get you out."

Agent Quan continued where Silvia left off, "In case any of you were wondering about how important these final tests are, only the surviving members of each team will go on to the final test. From there, only three of you will be invited to become part of DAWN."

"The teams will be distinguished by their coloured arm bands. Team Red is Adeline Jessie, Tom Apara, and Cassandra Viola. Your mission is to shut down the control tower." Silvia smiled at me for a second, and then addressed the other teams. Her wispy white hair fell over her shoulders and curled out. For the first time since I had arrived, I felt at odds with my body, trying to ignore the nervousness growing in my chest.

I didn't pay much attention to Silvia's instructions to the other teams.

A hand tapped my shoulder; I whisked around to look up at a tall, dark-skinned man with a round face and shaved head. He grinned, revealing deep dimples on each cheek. His fitted black shirt and combat pants revealed he was quite muscular, but then again, most of the initiates here were.

"Oh, hey, Tom."

He nodded. "Viola."

"Call me Vee," I replied.

Adeline walked up to join us, "Well, then you can call me Addy." Her high cheekbones and pale skin went perfectly with the thick golden braid hanging down her back. Addy slipped a red arm band on my upper arm. This was my team.

The heavy black doors before us opened, revealing a perfect little town built to scale. I guessed it probably spread about ten blocks from one end to the other, but it was hard to tell because of the darkness that enveloped us as we walked forward. The only light came from sporadically placed streetlights and the windows of a few dimly lit buildings. It was midnight according to the clock tower standing tall directly in the centre of the town, which explained the darkness. It was an impressive place.

"Oh, one more thing!" Agent Quan's voice bellowed through the speakers, "There are agents in black who will try to stop you. They are outfitted with the same equipment as you, so they can be shot at too. For the next couple hours, you will need to focus all your energy and astuteness on fulfilling your mission. Got it? Begin!"

People pushed past me, and for a second, I just stood there, still trying to process all the instructions. The anxiety that had begun building during Agent Quan's instructions had multiplied. I felt so out of control right now. Addy gently nudged me with her elbow.

"Let's go, Vee!"

I took a deep breath and started running with Tom and Addy. Maybe getting my blood flowing would help me shake off these nerves.

The town was made up of many old buildings, roads, and small houses eerily reminiscent of many of the small deserted towns across the country. The three of us snuck into the backyard of an abandoned house on a corner lot to discuss our plan.

Addy whispered a suggestion. "I think we should find the control tower by finding higher ground first, then we can identify its power source and see how we can disable it."

I interjected, "Good thinking, Addy, but first, we need to find weapons. I have a feeling there will be some strong resistance around that place."

Tom motioned for us to stay put and ran to the front of the house and back again, gesturing with his hand. "We need to get supplies from that building kitty-corner to us."

"How do you know for sure?" Addy asked, confused.

"Uh, I'm just taking a wild guess, but it's the building that says 'Armoury' on the front, Addy," he snickered.

"Well, I was just testing you." The deep blush on her cheeks added to her look of admiration. We cautiously made our way to the front of the house, using the same path Tom had taken. Our black clothes and boots blended in so well with the shadows that all anyone could see were three bright red arm bands floating in the air.

A single streetlight up ahead illuminated a masked black figure holding a large weapon. I squinted at the outline of the weapon: the front of the barrel was wide with green markings on it—the ghost blaster.

We pressed our backs against the brick wall.

Addy whispered, "Let's go the long way around to get to the back of that building."

The black figure didn't move as we stealthily sprinted down the alley until we could circle back without him noticing. Disappointment filled us as we snuck up to the back of the armoury and noticed there wasn't a back door.

"How do we get in?" Tom inquired. "The front door would be impossible!"

I pointed to the lone window to our right side on the back wall. If we couldn't get inside, we could at least get an idea of the layout through the small window. Addy and I crept up and peered in. A quick peek inside revealed several wooden crates, but otherwise, the room was empty. Shadows of black figures danced on the floor against the dim light shining in from the adjoining room.

As I turned away to find Tom, I caught sight of something flickering on the end of the wall a few feet from where we were standing. My brain told me it looked like a piece of metal embedded in the concrete, but I moved closer to investigate anyway. There was a reason it looked odd. I went to press my palm against the gray surface, and my hand passed right through that section of the wall. My jaw dropped open as I brought my hand back out and looked over at Tom and Addy. After an initial look of surprise, they did a silent celebration dance in the grass.

Stifling a giggle, I held my breath and walked through the wall. The hologram manipulated and bent the dim light, flashing in my eyes for a second before revealing the inside of the building.

Tom stuck his head through the wall and whispered, "Vee, grab some weapons and get out!"

Carefully, I opened one of the boxes. Inside were weapons streaked with green paint, identical to the weapon the masked figure out front was holding. They were longer and larger than pistols but lightweight in my hand when I picked one up. The front of the barrel was wide in diameter and could be rotated.

I could feel my heartbeat in my throat as I heard footsteps from the other room. Silently snatching three weapons, I swivelled on my heels and ran out.

I raced out into the night, and Tom and Addy followed close behind me. I glanced back to make sure no one had seen us. A huge smile broke out on Addy's face as she patted me on the back. We had escaped the armoury without being noticed.

I handed Tom and Addy their blasters, and we stopped behind a fence to examine our new toys and discuss our next move. There were only a few tall buildings in the town, including the clock tower. We decided to make our way to the tallest one; unfortunately, it was all the way across town. Even though the darkness helped keep us hidden, it also hindered us from moving as fast as we normally would have. Still, we thought it would be wiser to travel in the heavy shadows.

Skulking in the dark gave me an uneasy feeling. The only sound was Addy's and Tom's footsteps. I shushed them and they shushed me back. When all three of us thought we heard something in the distance, we slowed our pace so we could creep along even more quietly. We were on high alert. After some time had passed in silence, I turned to talk to my teammates.

"We need to communicate a little, or we'll lose each other," I whispered. Our footsteps were almost silent by now and being drowned out by my heart beating in my chest.

Addy's voice came from the right, "Tom, where are you?"

"I'm over here."

I opened my mouth to say something else, but a large gloved hand roughly clamped my mouth shut. I tried to scream, but the sound stayed in my throat, unable to escape.

"Vee?"

My heart skipped a beat as the attacker grabbed my arm with his other hand. Suddenly, my training kicked in, and that icy calmness flooded my body and my mind became razor sharp. Although my natural instinct was to drop my weapon and fight, my training told me to keep a death grip on my ghost blaster instead. Though I couldn't yell out, I still made plenty of scuffling sounds as I was dragged away from my friends. I kicked my legs but couldn't connect with anything. Finally, I pushed back the glove on my attacker's hand and dug my nails in as hard as I could. When I felt his grip loosen, I slammed the handle of my weapon backward, making contact with his torso.

"Oof." My assailant completely let go of my arm, and I stumbled a few steps away to get out of his reach. A deep, rumbling voice in the darkness threatened, "You can't escape me. I'll find you."

I straightened and turned around, raising my ghost blaster. The end of it butted up against the front of my shoulder and my finger was ready on the trigger. My eyes narrowed in search of my target, but I saw and heard nothing. The silence was deafening.

At that point, I knew I was alone. Tom and Addy were smart enough to run off, and I desperately hoped they hadn't lost each other in the chaos. I breathed slowly, trying to push down the fear growing in me. I needed to control it. The last thing I needed was to start panicking. My greatest fear, my one weakness, was being completely alone. I forced myself not to think about being abandoned and forgotten. This was a game, and I had to keep going. I manoeuvred toward the faint outline of the tallest tower, deciding to chance that it had to be the control tower. The confrontation had wasted time. I had to trust Addy and Tom were on their way there as well by now.

My stomach churned from the taste of blood in my mouth. I must have bitten down on my tongue while trying to wrestle away from the agent. My heart sped up when I heard rushing water. I slowed my pace to a walk until a stone fountain came into view. I realized I had entered a small park as there were no buildings nearby, only skinny birch trees and bare bushes. This was not a good place to stay hidden. I strained my eyes to make sure my route was clear and then pumped my legs as fast as I could. Faster, faster, faster!

I was desperate for this test to be over. I was desperate to not be alone. Hot tears blurred my vision. I wiped them away with my sleeve. I hated myself for crying.

The muscles in my legs ached and burned, and my lungs screamed for more oxygen. My whole body was begging me to stop, yet I willed myself to keep going.

"Almost there…almost there…almost there…" my brain chanted encouragingly as I matched my strides with the words.

When I finally arrived, I stopped and crouched down, taking long breaths to slow my heart rate. I scanned the entire area, looking for any signs of movement, but didn't notice anything. The building was dimly lit inside, and the entire structure looked about five stories high. The lowest windows I could see were on the second story. If I scaled the drainpipe, I could possibly climb through one. I secured my ghost blaster to my belt, got a good grip on the pipe with my right hand, hoisted myself up, and began to climb.

"Vee? Is that you?" a voice whispered loudly from below me. I glanced down and saw Addy's hopeful face. Tom was right behind her. Relief filled my body as I reached down to grab her outstretched hand.

"Guys," I gestured toward the window. "I think we can get in through there."

Addy secured her foot and began to clamber up the side of the building after me. Tom stayed on the ground, waiting until we could get ourselves through the window. We were pretty sure the pipe wouldn't hold all three of us at the same time. Addy grinned like she was having the time of her life.

The windowpane easily slid to one side. I was panting by the time I climbed through, finally realizing how exhausted I was. Hopefully, my adrenaline and training could keep me going until this was over. Addy hopped in right behind me, and a few seconds later, Tom jumped in and closed the window behind him. The room we landed in was tiny and bare, so after a quick glance out the door, we slipped into the corridor.

Masked guards in black patrolled the hallway, ghost blasters in hand. Three appeared at the end of the hallway coming toward us, forcing us to dart into the closest room we could find. As we pressed ourselves against the wall, we could hear them walking by and chatting about something that had caused all three members of the blue team to be eliminated.

The guards sauntered away, but we waited a few minutes to make sure no one had spotted us. When our eyes adjusted to the darkness and we were certain no one was there, Addy started rummaging around. We chalked it up to sheer luck when Addy discovered the room we had found refuge in contained masks, the exact kind all the other agents in black were wearing. As we slipped on the masks, I noticed they had green-tinted goggles. They made everything look a lot brighter. There were even holes for breathing through the mouthpiece.

Everything made more sense when I found the earpiece and the tiny mic woven into the lining of the mask. That was how they were communicating with each other. Tom grabbed a black t-shirt from a stack in the corner of the room, almost knocking down the whole pile. He reduced it to shreds in a matter of seconds and handed Addy and I each a piece of black fabric to wrap around our bright red arm bands. At first glance, no one would suspect we were different from any of the other guards wandering around.

Tom crouched to retie the laces on his boots. "Where do you think the control room is?" he asked in a hushed tone.

"My guess is they would choose a room on one of the top floors because it would be the hardest to get to," I whispered.

"We'll have to find the stairs, or maybe the elevators."

Addy quietly chimed in, "If I can gain access to the computers, I can shut the power off within a minute."

We each took a deep breath, straightened, and strode out as though we belonged there. We didn't draw any unwanted attention as we nudged each other toward the elevator doors that came into view. Nobody spoke the rest of the way up as we suspected there might be cameras on us. Tom jammed his thumb on the button for the fifth floor. We would start at the top.

After exiting the elevator, we lingered momentarily at the fascinating view offered by the floor-to-ceiling window that stretched from the elevator to the closest door.

Addy gasped, "It's beautiful!"

I agreed and added, "For an artificial town."

For some reason, Addy reminded me of Wren. Even though I had only known her for a short while, she seemed so familiar to me. As much as I didn't want to be eliminated from the test, and DAWN, I also hated the thought of her being eliminated as well.

Addy pulled me to the corner of the wall just outside the door of yet another room and gestured toward the words inscribed above the door: "Control Room." We were in the right place, and I hoped our plan would work, even though it had been hastily put together in the few short minutes we'd had to spare. We'd successfully overcome the obstacles in the first part of the test, and I refused to let myself think we wouldn't be just as successful now.

We pushed ourselves into the shadows as Tom burst through the door, yelling that he had seen us outside. He was very convincing, and I made a note to commend him on his acting skills later. It seemed almost too easy as three of the four guards in the room ran out with Tom, and Addy and I slipped inside, locking the door behind us. I strode over to the fourth guard sitting at the control desk and shot him in the back. The lights on his shoulders flashed as he froze in place. Addy and I threw off our masks since they weren't of any use now. Either we would fulfill our mission, or we would be caught trying.

"Sorry!" Addy shouted as the guard landed hard on the floor, still frozen, after she had shoved him out of his chair.

The control room walls were covered with computer screens showing footage from cameras set up around the town. The blue-green glow coming from the screens was the only source of light in the room.

Addy pushed back gold strands that had strayed from her braid and sat down in the rolling chair facing the main computer. "Uh, Vee, we have a problem. The computer needs a password. There's something in the background of the lock screen. I think it says, 'R-N-4-M-3 + B-L-U-3.'"

"Must be a hint," I concluded, then leaned over Addy's shoulder to study the letters and numbers. "R...ar, 'n,' four, 'm,' three, and blue." I muttered different variations under my breath.

Addy's brows furrowed. "We don't have a lot of time."

"Ar—our name!" I exclaimed, "Red plus blue is purple!"

Addy's fingertips flew over the keyboard so fast I barely had time to blink. "Yes!" She continued typing. She'd been right: it didn't even take her a minute. The screens went blank, and a robotic female voice announced over the intercom, "Mission complete."

"We did it!" Addy shouted as she jumped up and ran to the door, unlocking it to see Tom's grinning face, his hand up waiting for a high five.

"Well done." A voice came from behind us, making all three of us jump and spin around in shock.

Agent Quan appeared from the shadows in the corner of the room and approached us. He had been watching the whole time, and somehow, we hadn't seen him. He patted the ghost blaster pointed in our direction. "There is one last part I didn't mention. Only two members from each team can move on from this test. You must decide which team member will be eliminated."

The three of us stayed silent as we let his words sink in. The guard we'd shot earlier had recovered from his temporary paralysis and was leaning against the wall, watching us with interest.

I turned to see Addy shifting her weight to step forward, so I stepped in front of her to block her from moving.

All three of us exchanged worried glances, and I slowly wrapped my fingers around the handle of the ghost blaster hanging from my belt. I wasn't going to let anyone on our team go down without a fight.

"Well?" Agent Quan waved his ghost blaster at me impatiently. He sighed. "You have to choose. One of you has to get shot or all of you will be eliminated."

The next few moments went by so quickly I didn't have time to think about the consequences. In one motion, I grabbed my ghost blaster and shoved it against the side of Agent Quan's weapon, pinning him momentarily against the wall. His weapon was now aimed away from my team and just above my left shoulder. The surprise in his eyes told me he had not anticipated my actions.

"I choose you," I said in a steely cold voice.

Agent Quan's actions were swift, and I barely had time to fire my ghost blaster as he pushed me off and fired his weapon at my chest. The lasers disappeared into both of our suits. The flashing lights on his shoulders signalled he was dead, but I didn't have time to react before a jolt of unbelievable pain coursed through my entire body. My vision dimmed and my body went limp as the paralysis set in.

The temporary paralysis dissolved only a few moments later. Tom and Addy hadn't moved, and I looked over to see an angry Agent Quan pick himself up off the floor. He glared at me with piercing eyes and threatened, "Someday I'll make you pay for that."

With dejected but grateful looks on their faces, Tom and Addy silently mouthed a thank you as they followed the seething Agent Quan out of the building. They were going to continue on to the final test. I had no idea what or when that was happening, but I knew it wasn't going to involve me after my hasty sacrifice.

The guard we'd shot walked over to escort me out of the building after the others had gone. He had also ditched his mask, revealing a tousled mess of shoulder-length, dirty blonde locks and perfect, pearly white teeth.

He grinned, "That was totally awesome!"

I didn't reply as I gingerly stood up to follow him.

"Oh, by the way, I'm Tolli." The agent paused and looked at me, pride shining in his eyes. "Don't look so defeated! Despite being shot, you've been successfully recruited."

I furrowed my brow. That didn't make any sense. I'd been shot, so I was eliminated. That was the rule.

He must have noticed my confusion because he added, "Agent Mallick, our fearless leader, watched the entire thing. He saw you walk through the hologram and steal the weapons, fight off your attacker in the dark, and persevere even when you were separated from your team. He watched you figure out the computer's password, and then saw you sacrifice yourself when you stood up to Kyler and shot him." He burst into a fit of laughter at the mention of Kyler and had to stop walking to collect himself. I felt the blood rush to my face as I waited for him to finish laughing.

He chattered away as we walked, telling me about what had happened to the other teams and who had been eliminated. Surprisingly, "death" was not as humiliating as I had thought it would be. I listened to him politely but didn't feel like adding my own commentary to the events. My mind was still processing his words.

After a short walk, Tolli pushed open a side door hidden in the black wall and motioned for me to peek out. He pointed to a group of people and said, "Go that way as soon as they're gone. There's someone who wants to meet you. See you around, Agent Vee!" He confidently sauntered away, whistling a happy tune.

I squinted as my eyes adjusted to the bright light. A tall man with golden brown skin was giving instructions. The small round glasses resting on his nose softened his features, making him look friendly and approachable. He waved his hands animatedly as he spoke. "Thank you, everyone. That concludes this test. Since you are the small group of 'survivors,' you will need to follow Agent Quan to prepare for the final test," he explained before dismissing the small group. I caught a glimpse of Addy's blonde braid and Tom's shaved head as they walked in the opposite direction.

I tried to quietly shut the door behind me, but the click of the latch made the man look over in my direction. A warm smile appeared on his face when he spotted me. He darted over to me and grabbed my hand. "I'm Agent Mallick. It's great to finally meet you. Cassandra Viola, welcome to DAWN! I hope you'll feel at home here." Without any more explanation, he gave me a firm handshake and was gone in the blink of an eye.

Bewildered and confused, I looked around me. Only when I saw Silvia running toward me with her arms outstretched and a huge smile on her face, did I let the news sink in.

⇛ 10 YEARS, 1 MONTH, 15 DAYS, 13 HOURS, and 51 MINUTES to SILEO TERRA

April 12, 2060, 10:09 am...

It had taken me nearly a year to figure out who I was really working for. This government organization—DAIR—was solely in the business of developing advanced technology, and most importantly, its research was not suitable for public knowledge. That was where DAWN came in. This small division within the organization served as its protector. The entire DAIR facility was enormous; it contained aircraft hangers and massive laboratories, dining halls and living quarters, offices and theatres for large meetings, and DAWN's training facilities, where I had spent most of my last year. Although I knew the general layout of the entire place, I found myself discovering new and unusual places almost every day.

It was during one of these wanderings that I came face to face with her. I had been told to find Tolli and Donahue and tell them Agent Mallick needed to talk to them about Amelia, but since it wasn't urgent, I had decided to try a new route. My guess was that after six months of analysis, someone had finally figured out how to operate the mysterious contraption.

As I wandered through the massive complex, I found myself in a new hallway unfamiliar to me. I turned a sharp corner and came face to face with a russet-haired girl with implanted metal on her skin and an unmistakable green tint in her eyes. My heart stopped when I recognized her beautiful face. It looked different from what I remembered, but aside from the obvious changes, it only looked a little older. There was no denying her face belonged to my friend Wren.

I didn't know if I was overwhelmed with joy, grief, or shock. This was impossible. She returned my stare with her striking green eyes, and I inched closer.

"Wren? Is it really you?" My words barely escaped from my lips.

She bit her lip uneasily as I walked up to her. I couldn't believe it. Slowly, I reached out and touched her cold metal-coated hands. It felt like a dream, and I stared at her face until recognition blossomed in her eyes. She smiled and nodded at me. "Cass?"

I embraced her in a tight squeeze.

"I thought you were dead. I thought you were dead," I began to sob into her shoulder. Glistening tears streamed down my face.

I stepped back to make sure I wasn't dreaming. Metal bled from her face and scaled down the back of her neck. She was wearing jeans and a hoodie, so I couldn't see how much metal was attached to her body. She clutched my hands as hard as I was clutching hers.

She gently spoke to me, "Cass, I'm all right. My parents didn't...they didn't survive the accident, but I did. My uncle saved me with these robotics, and I've lived here ever since. He's...he's gone now too though."

For a few moments, we were both speechless. My mind raced, thinking back on all those years I had spent grieving her death. I had missed her so much, but now I had my friend back.

"Wren?" I had something important to tell her.

"Yeah?"

I smiled wearily. "Don't ever die again."

A giggle escaped her lips. "Okay, Cass, I promise."

9 YEARS, 7 MONTHS, 8 DAYS, 22 HOURS, and 22 MINUTES to SILEO TERRA

October 19, 2060, 1:38 pm...

Wren took a big bite of her BLT, causing the tomato juice to squirt onto my tray. She laughed with her mouth full as I jumped up to get some napkins. We were eating a late lunch in one of the facility's cafeterias. I grinned as I walked back to our table.

"Sorry!" Wren exclaimed.

"Let's try to be more proper," I said in my best English accent. That just made us start giggling more.

I sat back down and scooped a spoonful of beef barley soup into my mouth. I grabbed a handful of blueberries from the bowl we shared between us. As I popped berries into my mouth one at a time, I focused on the satisfying squish of sweetness that burst out with each bite. I realized I hadn't felt this happy in a long time. The six months since Wren and I had rediscovered our friendship had held more joy even than our time together as children. Maybe because we'd been given a second chance, and we'd learned the hard way how rare second chances were.

"We should keep these away from Donna," Wren remarked as she delicately took a blueberry out of the bowl. "They're his favourite."

"Yeah," I agreed. I smiled, remembering how Donahue had stolen Tolli's bowl of blueberries earlier as we'd sat down at their table.

I took a deep breath and changed the subject. "You know, you really don't need to confront Cyril."

Wren's lip twitched.

I pursed my lips as I thought about how dangerous Cyril was. I had no control over Wren's decision, but I still felt like I should protect her. "I mean, I know you stopped him from escaping, and that was amazing by the way—catching that bullet. But maybe you should just leave him for DAWN to handle."

Wren stared at her sandwich, absentmindedly playing with something in her pocket. "I don't know, I feel like he might know some things…"

"Oh, Wren, please don't go!" I couldn't help but imagine the worst outcome. "Are you talking about that machine he built? I can tell you everything I know instead. We retrieved it almost a year ago, and our scientists studied it for a while. It was based off some plans he stole from your uncle, but Cyril didn't build an exact prototype. His machine can open some kind of portal, but there's more to it than that. Our scientists hypothesized it could lead to another dimension but concluded it was too dangerous to activate. So, it's been locked up for a few months now just collecting dust. Cyril hasn't given us any useful information so far; he was probably counting on his escape to be successful. I wouldn't bet on him talking now either."

Wren changed the subject. "Do you know how he escaped?"

I sighed quietly and answered, "Surprisingly, he still had some pull with a few of his ex-colleagues."

She pushed herself up from the table in a huff. "I need to know what he knows," she mumbled over her shoulder on her way out.

For a brief moment, her eyes flashed a glowing blue, and I stared at her, trying to convince myself I was just dreaming. How could someone's eyes suddenly flash another colour?

⫷ 9 YEARS, 6 MONTHS, 15 DAYS, 23 HOURS, and 10 MINUTES to SILEO TERRA

November 12, 2060, 12:50 pm...

I knew it. I'd known in my gut Wren never should have confronted Cyril. I'd tried to convince her not to, but she'd done it anyway. Even though he'd been contained after his thwarted escape attempt, he'd still managed to push Wren too far. She'd flown into a rage, unleashing some crazy, unexplainable lightning power hidden within her. The power had cut out all the cameras in that part of the facility, so the only information we had now was what Cyril had told us. He'd rambled on and on about lightning coming from Wren's fingertips and how the lightning had struck Donahue, who was now in the infirmary in a coma. We had brought in the best doctors, but they were quite certain he would never wake up again.

We could get nothing from Wren. It was so hard to be around her. She was consumed by guilt for what she had accidentally done to Donahue, and her anger was out of control. Every time I had tried talking to her, she had just ended up yelling at me to leave her alone. She spent all her days locked in her room. Sometimes, I could hear her beating her fists against the walls. Other times, I would stand outside her silent room and stare at the strange blue glow coming from the bottom of her door. Agent Mallick had tried reaching out to her too, but he wasn't getting anywhere either.

I felt hopeless as I walked distractedly to see Donahue. It had become my daily ritual. It didn't feel right to leave him by himself. He didn't even have any family to call. I looked up to see Tolli walking out of Donahue's room; we solemnly nodded to each other. He spent most of his spare time in that room, sitting beside his best friend.

I walked in and glanced at Donahue lying peacefully on the bed. I took my normal seat beside the window, leaned my head back on the headrest of the armchair, and closed my eyes. There didn't seem to be a way out of this mess we were trapped in.

I must have drifted off because when I opened my eyes, an hour had gone by.

Sighing, I grabbed a book from the nearby coffee table and started skimming the pages.

"What in the world happened?" Donahue groaned, his voice hoarse from disuse.

9 YEARS, 6 MONTHS, 15 DAYS, 22 HOURS, and 20 MINUTES to SILEO TERRA

November 12, 2060, 1:40 pm...

Disoriented, Wren staggered backward, her hand still grasping her forehead.

"Wren?" Cautiously, I entered the room.

Wren's eyes were wide with terror and confusion, and her jaw gaped open as though her face was frozen. She moved back to get farther away from Donahue and me. He had managed to get himself out of the bed and stood next to me. Part of me felt bad that I'd raced him to Wren's room the minute he'd woken up from his coma, but I'd been so sure showing her Donahue was okay would be the solution.

I looked back at Wren. But we were too late.

"We're not going to hurt you," Donahue spoke slowly. "We just want to help you."

Wren cradled her head in her hands and murmured, "I don't know... I don't know. I can't remember...I need...I need someone." She set her a hand on a nearby table to steady herself, but her metallic fingers slipped, and she ended up crashing to the ground with a thud.

I rushed to her side, but I didn't know how to help or comfort her.

"Who do you remember?" I prompted her gently.

"My uncle...oh, no, no..."

I glanced at Donahue and then back at Wren. "Do you remember us at all?"

"I—I don't know you." Wren tried to stand but her wobbly legs couldn't support her weight. She sunk to her knees and lay down on the floor, curling up into a fetal position. I put my hand out to comfort her, but she swatted it away.

Her words cut deeply, and my heart hurt even more than when I'd been told she had died. I couldn't stand by and watch helplessly. "I'll go get Agent Mallick," I mumbled to cover up the emotions welling up inside my chest, and I turned to leave.

As soon as I left the room, I broke into a sprint, barely noticing the people I bumped into in my careless haste. Hot tears stung my eyes. Agent Mallick would be able to help undo the damage Wren had done. He would know what to do.

I flew past Tolli.

"Vee, what's the matter?" he yelled after me.

I didn't have time to stop and explain, so I kept running, but he scrambled after me and caught up. I was panting hard, but I managed to breathe out, "Wren erased her memory. I need to find Agent Mallick, now."

Suddenly, Tolli reached out and grabbed my arm, causing me to lose my balance and smash into him. He caught me and swung us both around to face the other direction. I glared at him and was about to tell him exactly what I thought of him when he yelled, "He's that way!"

I followed him down the hallway until we saw Agent Mallick walking out of the dining room munching on a pear. When he saw us barreling toward him as fast as we could, he threw his hands out to stop me from crashing into him, losing his pear and sending it flying into the air. I leaned over to catch my breath for a second before blurting out all the details about Wren and the memory eraser in one panicked sentence after another.

I gulped down more air. "Please, Agent Mallick, you need to help her."

We raced back to Wren's room, where we found her curled up in the corner. She was tearing at her hair in frustration, and Donahue was trying to help, but she wouldn't let him near her.

Tears welled up in his eyes as he whispered repeatedly, "Wren, you know me."

"Go away," she hissed.

Agent Mallick gasped when he saw Donahue and ran over to embrace him. Donahue teetered unsteadily. Tolli was only a second behind him, running to his best friend. I suddenly realized that in all the confusion I had forgotten to mention to either of them that Donahue had come out of his coma. Donahue was so weak that he collapsed against Agent Mallick. Tolli and Agent Mallick positioned themselves on either side of him to help him back to his bed outside the door. Both men tossed quick, worried glances back at Wren—who was still lying on the ground—as they staggered over to the bed.

I bent over Wren so I could look directly into her eyes and gently said, "Wren, do you remember anything that happened today?" To my surprise, she clasped onto my wrist.

"Don't, that hurts," she responded through gritted teeth. Wren tightened her grip, causing my fingers to start feeling cold with the lack of blood circulation. Her eyes were distant, and there was something about her voice that was unrecognizable. "You're hurting me," she said again, even though it was the other way around.

I clenched my teeth as the metal of her hands dug into my wrist, and I tried to wrestle my arm out of her grasp. I cried out as her metal thumb drew blood.

Agent Mallick raced back into the room and placed his thin, strong brown fingers over her hand. "Wren, let go. She's your friend."

She furrowed her brow and didn't reply, but she released her grip and shoved me away in one motion. I grabbed my wrist in pain. I felt it best to leave her with Agent Mallick, so without a word, I walked out of the room, applying pressure to the gash on my wrist. I felt empty.

Tolli and Donahue were waiting outside. Donahue was lying down on his bed staring at the ceiling, and Tolli fidgeted beside him. I set my hand on Donahue's shoulder but remained silent.

"We'll fix this," assured Tolli. "I know we will."

Tolli and I waited outside for hours as different doctors came in to try to help Wren. Donahue had been taken back to his room so they could examine him too. Their initial assessment of Wren concluded most of her recent memories had been erased, but we weren't sure if it was permanent. However, one thing seemed certain: Wren would never be the same again.

3 YEARS, 11 MONTHS, 7 DAYS, 9 HOURS, and 28 MINUTES to SILEO TERRA

June 20, 2066, 2:32 pm...

"It's nicer down here today," Donahue remarked.

The old warehouse had an underground level that was pleasantly cool on hot days. We'd lived without any luxuries, including an air conditioner, for six years now. I spread a ratty blanket on the concrete floor so we had a semicomfortable place to plan and discuss our options.

"Remember the good old days?" Tolli asked absentmindedly, leaning back on the blanket.

"I remember." Donahue smiled sadly and said, "We were happy. Wren was okay."

I sighed. My mind wandered from Wren to my mom and dad. "Wren was closer than family to me. My own parents are out there somewhere, living far away from each other. They don't even know where I am."

"At least your parents aren't in jail," Tolli put in. "My brother's probably there too."

Donahue remained silent for a while, but eventually he mumbled, "Aren't we a sad bunch? I can barely remember my family: Baba, Mama, and two brothers I never met. They're all gone now."

I placed a gentle hand on Donahue's shoulder. "But we have each other, and we have a plan—that we now need to alter—but it's still a plan. And we're still going to make it work." I gritted my teeth in determination. "What are our options now?"

The bubble shield had screwed up our plans. Time wasn't the big problem anymore. The time machine could fix everything; we just needed to make sure the rest of the plan worked. We wouldn't get another chance.

"So, we still can't kill her," Tolli said. "That's just not what we do. That's not what DAWN would have done. Besides, she's gained so many unnatural powers. No one can stand up to her right now, but we could still go back in time and confront her there."

"We aren't killing her past self either," Donahue concluded firmly. "It could change the timeline and cause major damage to our world. Think about it. We know the past shouldn't be altered, but maybe it could pause or something, so it doesn't cause a blank space in the timeline."

"So, would it freeze?" I asked.

"That's what I think would happen." Donahue dug out some crumpled paper from his pocket. "According to my calculations, the timeline could support itself for a while if a person removed themselves from it and travelled to the past to remove someone else. I believe we would have time, albeit limited time, to bring past Wren back to the present."

I protested, "But maybe we really should just try to kill her ourselves? Future Wren, I mean. As awful as it sounds, it may be the only way."

"Even if we wanted to, we can't; the odds are far too stacked against us," Tolli reminded me. "Teleportation, enhanced intelligence, lightning-quick reflexes," he listed each of Wren's growing abilities on his fingers, "unmatchable strength, manipulating gravity, and of course, the lightning. She'd probably kill us on sight if she thought we were a threat."

We had witnessed some of those powers. We had already been aware of her superhuman strength and high intelligence, but when the bubble shield was being constructed, Tolli decided to go in for a closer look and discovered Wren was blinking in and out of existence, or in other words, teleporting.

I reminded the guys, "Her headquarters are heavily guarded. We have to find a way to get in there, and through the shield, if we go with your plan, Donahue."

He nodded and lay down on his back, slipping his hands under his head.

"What if we just destroyed the generator? We wouldn't have to worry about the bubble shield then," Tolli suggested. "Oh, did you end up getting the plans, Vee?"

"Yeah, I got 'em." I had managed to follow a maintenance worker inspecting the shield a few days ago and scanned a copy of his blueprints. "The problem is it's impenetrable."

Donahue perked up, "I have some ideas."

Tolli laughed, "You always have ideas, and your ideas are crazy."

Donahue simply recited, "*Nullum magnum ingenium sine mixture dementia fuit.* That's Latin for 'There has been no great wisdom without an element of madness.'"

Smiling, I asked, "By the way, how close are you to getting the time machine to work?"

"Its name is Tempus III," Donahue corrected.

⇛? YEARS, ? MONTHS, ? DAYS, ? HOURS, and ? MINUTES to SILEO TERRA

Unknown date, unknown time...

Tempus III rattled loudly. Thunder and lightning swept across the sky, and vibrant pinks, purples, and wisps of blues mixed and intertwined like string being abstractedly knit together. We were hopeful this improved model could actually do what it was designed to do. We had done everything we could to make our first expedition back in time a success. From there, we could freeze past Wren's timeline momentarily and make things right.

It sounded straight forward in my mind, but we all knew the huge risks involved with such a mission.

When Wren had merged with the orb, she had become the most powerful being in the world, and she'd used her power to make the world her own. With the powerful orb and her robotics, she had acquired superhuman skills that were unmatched. Her eyes, now permanently blue, were a constant reminder the orb had taken its place within her. Life as we'd known it had ceased to exist as everything and everyone was forced to bend to Wren's will to create a secure environment for her...or it. Unfortunately, Wren's ideal world was not a comfortable place to live for anyone else but her, and it had continued to get worse as she desperately tried to gain more and more control and establish more and more security. It wasn't like anyone could stop her.

At first, everyone had thought of her as a saviour, but then her obsession with security grew. Her laws were heavily enforced, and the slightest opposition was eliminated. The people lived lives of incarceration, whether in prison or in their own homes. The laws included a curfew, zero tolerance for crime, and regulated lives with no freedom or privacy.

"What are we doing?" I mumbled under my breath. "How are we going to stop her?" I asked as I took my seat at the control desk.

"Only she can stop herself," Donahue anxiously reminded us. I looked at him, studying the grim expression on his face.

Wren had inadvertently destroyed DAWN when she had snuck away from Agent Mallick in her confused state after using the memory eraser on herself. Even with around-the-clock monitoring, she had found a way to slip away and find her time machine. Then she had tried to go back in time using Tempus II, and that had created the chaos.

The orb had caused another time storm, but this time, the storm had merged the orb with Wren instead of sending her to another time. The power surge that had resulted from the fusion had taken the lives of everyone inside the building and fried every electrical component and weapon we owned, except for a few scraps of electrical equipment and prototypes in the underground area. All that remained of any transportation was the single vehicle Tolli and I had been driving that day. We'd been lucky to have gotten Wren's plans for her time machine, but it had been difficult to find the equipment and supplies we needed to rebuild it. So, in the end, it had taken us longer than we had ever intended to get to where we were now.

Now, eleven years later, our only mission was to fix her mistakes.

"Donahue, you should smile more. You look like you're about to murder someone," I remarked, trying to lighten the mood.

"No promises, Vee." Tolli and Donahue answered in unison, and this time, we all smiled.

One of the early ideas we had considered for our mission was to go back in time and eliminate Wren before she had merged with the orb, but we knew if we didn't return her to her present, we were risking a change in the timeline we would have no control over. Any actions that could alter the timeline that drastically were far too dangerous as the consequences could be catastrophic to the future. It was one of the main rules of time travel, and we knew we needed to abide by its wisdom. So instead, our plan had shifted to briefly borrowing her younger self to make a few important changes to her older self.

I picked at my black suit, twisting the tight cuffs around my wrists. I looked down at my olive-toned skin and ran my finger over the scar I had received the last time I'd seen Wren.

Deep down, I was terrified of our mission, but outwardly, I remained calm and collected, as usual.

PART FOUR
TREVOR TOLLI

≋ 20 YEARS, 9 MONTHS, 24 DAYS, 7 HOURS, and 45 MINUTES to SILEO TERRA

August 3, 2050, 4:15 pm...

The beach was pleasant at this time of year, unlike the cool winds that would descend on it in about a month. Right now, it was the perfect place to sit in the sand for hours, chatting with my older brother, Aaron, or staring off into the horizon when we needed to rest our minds. We could build sandcastles, skip rocks, or swim to the closest sandbar if we wanted to burn off some energy. This place was truly a getaway vacation spot, and it was only an hour away from Ashborne. Aaron had just received his driver's licence earlier this summer, only three days after his sixteenth birthday, so we often took off to spend the day here. I hoped he would never get tired of letting me tag along with him, especially because I wouldn't be able to get my own licence for another four years.

Aaron sighed beside me, "I wish summer lasted forever." He brushed back his golden-blonde curls, accidentally sprinkling sand in his hair in the process. "But someone needs to be The Ace, the Greatest Entertainer Ever."

"You can't keep The Ace hidden from the world," I agreed.

Aaron called himself "The Ace" when he did his amateur magic shows because his specialty was card magic. My parents and I liked calling him Ace as well because it suited his personality. He always carried a few packs of cards in his pockets, and he practised his tricks on me all the time. My favourite trick was the one called Four Aces. The deck was shuffled in a precise way and split into four piles. Everything lined up in the end. Tada! Four aces on top of four piles. The trick was simple, and even though it was one of the few tricks Ace had shown me how to do, it was my favourite because it was the first one I remembered us spending hours practising together.

"Remember when you tried Four Aces on me the first time? You didn't even get one ace on top of the pile." I laughed.

Summer break was always the best part of the year. This one was going to be the best one yet because Ace and I planned to spend all our days by the lake doing absolutely nothing. At this time of the year, the sun wouldn't completely set until close to midnight. Still, soft pink and orange hues shone on the horizon in the summer evening sky. A refreshing breeze pushed my blonde hair into my face. There was no better moment, there was no better time, and there was no better place. I leaned back on my towel and savoured it all.

"I wish summer lasted forever," Ace repeated.

It was the peace and tranquility we loved the most. The water on the shore slapped the sand repeatedly at my feet. I stood up and started skipping stones on top of the glassy surface. Plunk! Plunk! Plunk!

Ace's gaze drifted along the shore of the lake. Absentmindedly, he shuffled a deck of cards in one palm. "I don't think I could wish for much more than this."

"Agreed."

"Trevy?! Did you just *agree* with *me*?" he asked, using an annoying, exaggerated tone.

"What? No."

Out of the corner of my eye, I could faintly see a figure hurrying down the beach. His footsteps made little noise as they touched the wet sand. It was my cousin, Gage. I waved my arms and exclaimed, "Hey, Gage is here! Did you tell him to come, Ace?" As he got closer, I could see the sweat dripping down the sides of his face, causing his thick, straight brown hair to stick to his forehead.

"What's up, Gage?" Ace asked, rising from his towel and dusting off the sand that had collected on his swim trunks.

He bent down and rested his palms on his knees to catch his breath. "The cops…they came to your house. They just arrested your parents!"

9 YEARS, 6 MONTHS, 11 DAYS, 15 HOURS, and 37 MINUTES to SILEO TERRA

November 16, 2060, 8:23 am...

Agent Mallick was urgently trying to find out all he could about the development of the memory-erasing technology. It was so new, it hadn't even been approved for testing yet. We needed knowledge beyond our own doctors and scientists to help Wren, so he'd chosen to send Vee and I on a quick mission.

We were to travel to Ashborne to see an old colleague of Agent Mallick's. He had given us her name and address: *Dr. Jennifer Davis, 2004 Cobblestone Avenue.* She had retired from DAIR many years ago, but she had been an integral part of the organization, specifically in the neurology department. Agent Mallick hadn't been able to contact her, so he'd asked us to find her. If we could track her down and convince her to help us, she would be packing her bags and staying at our facility once again.

I was looking forward to putting a little distance between myself and the stressful situation we were leaving behind. Donahue was recovering well, but he was frustrated he still needed to use a wheelchair to get around, even though he'd only come out of the coma a few days ago. Also, he was particularly anxious about Wren's condition, which even with Agent Mallick's attention and care and DAIR's seemingly endless resources, wasn't changing much.

It was good to have something to focus on instead of sitting around twiddling our thumbs. Besides, Vee and I were excited to try out this new mode of transportation being developed by some of our engineers.

It had a long, sophisticated name, but most of us referred to it as "The Wheel" because it resembled a giant wheel with two small seats, one in front of the other. The outside rotated like a wheel, but the middle, or "hub," stayed put. The controls in the front were quite simple, consisting only of a brake and a gas pedal. Instead of a steering wheel, there was a handle on each side of the front seat to control the vehicle's direction, and The Wheel was light enough that leaning one's body to one side or the other helped it turn more sharply. The thin lining surrounding the exterior was controlled by an automatic camo-adapter, allowing the lining to act as a cloaking device for the entire apparatus. The lining even supported thousands of miniature cameras and screens, enabling the vehicle to blend into its surroundings. The occupants inside could see out clearly, but anyone outside wouldn't notice it apart from the faint whir of the engine. Of course, The Wheel hadn't been perfected yet; this was only the first prototype, but that made it even more exciting to try.

Vee opened the side door of The Wheel and motioned for me to climb into the backseat. I didn't argue because she always refused to let anyone else drive. I jumped in and made myself comfortable as I looked around and grinned.

The journey to Dr. Davis' would take us about two hours, which would have been reduced significantly if we had been allowed to travel on the highway. But alas, that had been strictly forbidden. Even though the ride through the forested areas was quite bumpy, the upside was there was no traffic.

"Vee, do you think Wren will be okay?"

She didn't reply and kept her focus on manoeuvring the handles. We spent the rest of the ride in silence.

We stopped The Wheel near the edge of the city before the trees around us disappeared. We could see the north side of Ashborne, and from where we were parked, it would be an easy jaunt in to catch a cab.

Suddenly, dark clouds started collecting above us and drowning out the sunlight. We heard the faint but unmistakable deep rumble of thunder that grew stronger by the second.

"Odd," I remarked. "Thunderstorms don't usually happen that fast."

The Wheel's radio transmitter beeped twice just before we exited the vehicle. Vee and I exchanged glances as she spoke into the small speaker, "Vee here. What's up?"

The speaker crackled and then we heard Donahue's panicked voice. "You guys need to come back now! She's gone insane and the lightning and the storm..."

"Donahue, what in the world are you talking about?"

The speaker went silent for a second. Then he screamed, "Come back now!"

The storm clouds had completely dispersed by the time Vee and I arrived back at the government facility a few hours later. Donahue was sitting outside in his wheelchair waiting for us. The front doors of the building were missing, and it looked like something had blown the entrance apart.

We jumped out of The Wheel and raced over to Donahue, who was pale and shivering uncontrollably. A flash of anger burned through me. Donahue was still recovering from the coma, and he didn't need to be worrying about anything right now. I didn't understand why he would have been left alone in his condition.

"Wren..." he stuttered, "And the orb...something happened." I placed my hand on his shoulder to try to calm him down. Donahue gestured to the building, "There was lightning inside but it...it didn't affect her. It was almost as if...as if it knew her, as if it *was* her."

"You mean she controlled the storm?" I questioned.

Vee glared at me and raised her voice, "Wren would never do that!"

"I didn't say she did! But you have to remember, she has barely any memories and no control over herself. The orb did something. She's not herself; she's not Wren!" Donahue yelled.

Vee and I snapped our heads toward him in synchronicity, surprised by the inference of his words and the sudden strength of his outburst.

He spun around before we could say anything else and wheeled himself back into the complex. Vee and I exchanged confused looks and shrugged as we followed him in.

≋ 9 YEARS, 6 MONTHS, 11 DAYS, 11 HOURS, and 55 MINUTES to SILEO TERRA

November 16, 2060, 12:05 pm...

I had known it wasn't going to be good when Donahue had contacted Vee and I in hysterics. He had begged us to return home, so Vee had immediately turned our vehicle around. We didn't speak much during the long ride back. Vee just drummed her fingers on the handles and stared straight ahead. Even though we hadn't pressed Donahue for a clearer explanation, nothing could have prepared us for what we were about to walk into.

So much had happened in the last month. Cyril had tried to escape and then been recaptured. Then Wren had somehow accidentally put Donahue in a coma. Surprisingly, Donahue had recovered but not in time to stop Wren from erasing most of her memories. This had been such an overwhelming and heartbreaking time for all of us. I hoped there wasn't more to come.

When we finally got back to DAWN, we followed Donahue into the facility and witnessed the results of the tragic massacre. Bodies littered the entire building, but eerily, there was no blood. The only visible wounds on the bodies were dark burns and red jagged marks that mirrored the shape of the strange blue lightning that had spread destruction throughout the facility. We didn't see any movement aside from the random twitching limb from the nerve damage brought on by the mass electrocution. Not one person who'd been inside the building had been spared...except Wren Derecho.

Vee and I walked through the halls in shock. So many innocent lives had been taken today. I shook my head in disbelief. Our entire organization had been destroyed. My shock turned to grief as I recognized Agent Mallick lying on the ground. I ran to him, dropped to my knees beside his body, and sobbed.

I pounded the ground angrily with my fists and yelled at the top of my lungs, "NO, NO, NO, NO!" I buried my face in my hands. "No."

Something broke inside me at that moment. I'd had my share of pain and loss, but this was too much. Vee quietly knelt beside me, tears streaming down her face. She gently closed Agent Mallick's eyes, replacing his cracked glasses that had fallen on the floor.

As we continued down the hallway, it didn't take us long to find Vee's good friend and mentor, Agent Mercier. Vee rushed to the cold, lifeless body and held it close as great sobs wracked her thin frame. Vee's haunting, broken voice echoed off the empty walls as she cried out her dead friend's name. Gently but firmly, I pulled her away from Agent Mercier's body when she began to shake the body violently in a desperate attempt to wake her up. Agent Mercier's white hair fell over her face as Vee finally released her grip.

We kept walking in silent disbelief until we came upon Cyril. He had died in his prison with his eyes wide open and a grin plastered to his face as if this had been his plan all along. His hair was no longer perfectly slicked back but spiked and scorched, and his scar had burst open again.

⇛ 9 YEARS, 6 MONTHS, 8 DAYS, 10 HOURS, and 25 MINUTES to SILEO TERRA

November 19, 2060, 1:35 pm...

"**W**e need a plan," Vee stressed. Impatiently, she tapped her fingers on the desk in front of her.

Donahue was pacing back and forth while I stood in the middle of the room watching him. He was no longer in his wheelchair, not because he didn't need it, but because he refused to use it anymore.

We couldn't stay in the DAIR facility much longer. Wren hadn't reappeared since Donahue had seen her merge with the orb three days ago. We weren't sure if she would return, but we knew she'd seen Donahue alive before she left.

"We don't want to use violence," Vee started.

Donahue muttered, "Still, we need to do something about Wren."

Although he had good reason to be angry with her, his heart was still broken over losing her. I agreed with him, "Donahue's right. We don't know what she's capable of. She has to be stopped."

Anxiously, Donahue picked at the calloused skin on his hand, and even though he looked like he was ignoring me, I knew the gears in his head were spinning.

"I have an idea, but it's going to cost us."

"What are you suggesting?" I asked, intrigued.

"It's going to take us a really long time. I'm talking years." He ran his fingers through his dark hair and looked at me to gauge my reaction.

"We have time," I assured him and motioned for him to continue.

"Yes, we have time. And we can use that," Donahue mumbled.

Vee jumped up impatiently, "Stop being so cryptic and tell us what you're thinking."

"Time travel." Determination shone in his eyes. "Wren's time machine is upstairs. It's damaged beyond repair, but maybe we could take out some of the main components and try to rebuild it."

"Donahue, you want to rebuild it after it most likely caused all this, all this damage, all this death?" Vee asked doubtfully.

He slowly nodded his head and replied, "We'll have to actually make it work this time, then we come up with the best plan to avoid this part of the timeline."

"You mean, we reset the timeline?" I asked.

Vee sighed, "You guys, we really have to think about this. There are a million scenarios where this could end in an irreversible disaster."

We started brainstorming.

"What if the timeline collapses while we're travelling through it?!" I exclaimed. "I really don't feel like getting crushed while hurtling through another dimension."

Donahue bit his lip. "Maybe the past just needs to be altered a tiny bit."

"Would time correct itself, or would we start all over again?" Vee asked. "We could make the same mistake over and over again."

"Maybe, but maybe not..." Donahue's voice drifted off.

I sighed loudly, "And if we fail?"

"I need to think about this some more." He rubbed his forehead, deep in thought.

Donahue seemed to play this game on an entirely different level than us; in fact, he was the most intelligent person I had ever met, and I often marvelled at his ideas and sheer brain power. But I kept that to myself. No point in my friend getting a big head.

"But the bottom line is there's only one person I know who can help us." Donahue concluded.

"Who?!" Vee and I demanded in unison.

"Why, Wren Derecho, of course."

We looked at him blankly. I had no idea how our current enemy could be our only ally, our only solution.

Donahue stopped pacing and looked at us. He said firmly, "We travel to the past. It's a last resort, just like Rob said."

9 YEARS, 6 MONTHS, 7 DAYS, 19 HOURS, and 51 MINUTES to SILEO TERRA

November 20, 2060, 4:09 am...

"I can carry the rest of it, Donahue."

The three of us had spent the last fourteen hours working tirelessly to gather and transport all of Tempus II's vital components required for the rebuild. We had already relocated the fried hard drive, along with all Wren's designs and blueprints. Now we were almost finished transferring all the construction materials and tools we wouldn't have access to anywhere else.

Our new home was an abandoned warehouse Vee had told us about. It was located about an hour and a half's drive from the facility, but only about twenty minutes from the outskirts of Ashborne. Its seclusion created the perfect place for us to hide. Vee had remembered it from one of her exploring trips as a lonely teenager and had checked it out to make sure it was still empty.

We still had The Wheel, which we were grateful for even though the two seats weren't ideal for three people; however, it hadn't taken us long to come up with a good plan. We had decided Vee and I would gather supplies at the facility, and Donahue would drive back and forth. Vee was hesitant, but she had agreed. She'd known Donahue didn't have enough energy to run all over the building retrieving things. All Donahue had to do was unload everything in a pile and come back for the next load. He would do a final walk-through on the last trip to make sure we had all the supplies and tools we needed. We lost count of how many trips he took throughout the night, and we had to fight hard against the exhaustion that threatened to overtake us if we stopped for even a moment.

Suddenly, the endless hours were over, and we looked at each other with relief. Vee jumped into The Wheel with Donahue and they sped away. I took a couple hours to rest my eyes before Donahue returned one last time to do the final sweep. Meanwhile, Vee would move everything into the warehouse. Donahue was walking faster now, but I was still worried about the toll this last week had taken on his body. We started throwing odds and ends we thought we might need in a box, and I carried it, crammed with random parts, out of the room. As much as I loved this place, I was glad to leave it behind.

A minute later, I became aware Donahue wasn't following me, so I spun around in concern. He was standing outside Wren's now half-emptied room. I could almost see his memories draining the life out of him. His eyes were heavy with sorrow, and I could see how much pain and regret he was feeling over his failure to foresee and save Wren from her fate.

"Come on," I urged. There was nothing I could do now except keep him on track. "I may be carrying all this stuff, but you need to help me fit everything into The Wheel."

My voice jolted him out of his trance, and he jogged to catch up to me. We walked through the empty hallways and out the jagged hole in the front of the building.

When we got to The Wheel, we started cramming the supplies under the backseat as though we were solving a jigsaw puzzle. It didn't all fit, so I would have to carry the rest on my lap. I was about to climb in when Donahue stopped me. "What about Amelia?"

"What about Amelia?" I asked, looking at him blankly.

"I wonder if she would come in handy." Without waiting for a reply, he whirled around and dashed back toward the building. With a huge sigh, I ran after him, wondering if we were ever going to be fully rid of this godforsaken place.

"Do you even know where it is?" I asked as we raced to the underground part of the complex.

"Yeah, I was the one who locked it up, Tolli," Donahue replied as we turned a corner and stopped in front of a door with a number pad next to it.

Donahue pushed open the door without bothering with the code. We already knew the lightning blast had knocked out the entire security system, but we were relieved to find the concrete walls of the underground area protected a few rooms, so everything inside was undamaged. Amelia sat in the middle of the room. The metal claws, the circular disc perched atop the control box, and its long lever—everything it seemed—were all intact. Donahue wheeled it out, and we heaved it up the stairs to ground level. Although the machine was heavy, it was still manageable.

We had just reached ground level when a shriek from the floor above startled both of us. I jumped out of my skin, and Donahue almost tumbled back down the stairs but grabbed the railing and managed to catch his balance.

"WHAT HAPPENED TO MY TIME MACHINE?!"

"Donahue, hate to rush you, but we need to leave!" I whispered urgently.

Heavy footsteps pounded upstairs, rumbling the whole ceiling. Donahue lifted a finger to his lips, and we slowly began to tiptoe our way to the front door. A clatter up ahead stopped us dead in our tracks. How could she have been upstairs one minute, and ahead of us the next?

A sudden wave of fear hit me as I came to a realization. "Did Wren just jump off the second floor?"

"Shh!"

Quickly, we pushed Amelia into the nearest room to avoid being noticed. The room happened to be one of the many storage rooms in the building. This one looked like it had been used by the maintenance crew as there were hundreds of boxes housing different cleaning supplies and tools all lined up neatly on the dark brown shelves. Donahue and I pressed our backs against the wall, hoping we could remain hidden in the shadows. We slowly inched behind some cardboard boxes filled with rolls of paper towels.

I counted to thirty and then peeked slightly over the box I was crouched behind. At this angle, I could barely make out Wren's shadow through the crack in the door. She was pacing back and forth, tugging on her auburn locks and muttering to herself, "Time machine, time machine, time machine."

Wren was blocking our exit, so we had to be patient. My heart pounded in my chest, and I found myself taking shallow breaths. I glanced at Donahue, and his eyes were wide with concern. We both knew we wouldn't be able to simply walk away if Wren found us.

Under his breath, Donahue murmured, "I think there's an emergency exit in the corridor beside us." Then he pointed to the opposite side of the room. At the very back was a single door, camouflaged behind a few more cardboard boxes.

Carefully, we weaved our way to the back of the storage room. If Wren decided to peek in now, we would be dead. I heard her stomping up and down the hallway, her feet slamming against the ground in frustration. I shuffled the cardboard boxes out of our way, relieved their contents didn't move the slightest bit. Donahue eased the door ajar and squeezed through, looking to make sure the route was clear, and then held it open wider to allow me to wheel Amelia out.

We slipped into the corridor and saw the red exit sign clearly marked at the end of it. As we raced toward it, the wheels on Cyril's machine started squeaking. Donahue and I exchanged worried looks as I slowed down. We made it to the exit after a few heart-pounding seconds, and he silently opened the exit door so I could go through first.

I was so relieved to be out of the building, I made a promise to myself that I would never return, regardless of the circumstances.

We had exited out of the left side of the facility, putting us as far as possible from The Wheel. Now we had to sneak all the way around the back, without being caught, to where Donahue had parked The Wheel at the edge of the property. The adrenaline pumping through our bodies pushed us as we raced to our destination and lifted the heavy machine, dumping it down on the back seat. Right away, we both saw there was a problem.

"How are we gonna fit?!" I climbed into the front seat, and Donahue pushed me over to squeeze in next to me, but the door wouldn't close.

Panicked, I whispered, "Get on my lap!"

"What?!"

"Just do it!" I ordered as Donahue awkwardly perched on my lap, his legs pinned up against the front of the vehicle. I couldn't see anything in front of me, but I moved my foot around until I felt it step squarely on the gas pedal.

"Okay, I'm going to count to three. Then you accelerate as fast as you can, and I'll steer us into the tree line up ahead. If we make it past there, she won't be able to see or hear us," Donahue softly directed.

I didn't allow myself to think of what would happen if we failed. We couldn't leave Vee out there in the warehouse on her own.

"One."

Donahue started the vehicle, which impressively made no noise at all, and I readied my foot above the gas pedal.

"Two."

I held my breath.

"Three."

The machinery hummed as I slammed down on the pedal. The Wheel jerked forward and we were off.

Donahue's bony elbow dug into my jaw as he tried steering with little room to move.

"Ow! Watch your arms! I can't see a thing! You're gonna have to tell me what to do!" I hissed.

I glanced over my shoulder, and out of the corner of my eye, I saw lightning inside the building. Then I could just make out Wren's petite figure as she walked outside. Electric sparks danced around her, and her fists were clenched at her side. I slowly let my breath out as I saw her turning away from us. She hadn't spotted us with the cloaking device activated.

"Tolli, go, go, go!" Donahue slammed his foot down on top of my boot and we sped forward.

"Ease your foot up! I can't push on the pedal any harder than I already am," I complained, trying to keep my voice down. I still couldn't see anything with Donahue's gray shirt flapping in my face.

"We're so close, only a few more seconds."

I didn't know if it was his bones or his robotics, but I felt something dig sharply into my leg. I yelped. "Whose idea was this?!"

"Yours!" Donahue retorted and then he yelled, "Look out!"

The Wheel suddenly lurched upward, and we caught air. By the sound of it, we had hit a large bump. The impact made The Wheel turn sharply to the right, and our weight made it veer to the right even more.

"Off course!" Donahue yelled, panicking.

"Lean left!" I hollered back.

We shifted all our weight to the left to stop The Wheel from toppling over. We had barely steadied ourselves when I saw the dense trees approaching us to the side.

Soon, we found ourselves deep in the forest, but I kept checking behind me to make sure we weren't being followed. After travelling for about an hour, our breathing had slowed, and our focus had shifted to getting back to the warehouse. However, just when we felt we were in the clear, The Wheel's pedals started to stick. I took turns pressing on both pedals, but they weren't reacting to my touch. I desperately pressed my foot down repeatedly.

"Donahue, the pedals are stuck! I don't have control!" I shouted.

"What did you do?!"

"I didn't do anything!" My throat had started to hurt from all the hollering we had done earlier, so I added, "I guess we can stop yelling. Wren's long gone." I spared one more glance back and was relieved to not see anyone.

Donahue tensed at my words. He didn't reply. He tried to shift his position to stretch out his legs, but all he accomplished was to dig his metal brace into my shin. I grunted in pain and wondered if he'd done that on purpose, but I decided not to say anything about it.

Through gritted teeth I said, "I don't think we can stop this thing unless we crash it."

He nodded his head in agreement as the engine revved up on its own. Another lunge forward sent his shoulder blade crashing back into my chest.

"Ouch!"

"Lean as hard as you can to the left. We gotta knock this thing over," Donahue commanded.

Clumsily, we shifted all our weight against the left side and held tight onto the handles. The Wheel slowly tipped and began turning in circles, getting lower and lower to the ground each time around. I heard the sad crunching of pieces ripping off, followed by an irritating whirring.

"Just a little bit more," Donahue encouraged in a strained voice.

As we slipped down further, the momentum pressed my body against the side door and pushed Donahue back against me, constricting my lungs. With a final, slow spin, the vehicle collapsed and slid against the ground, wobbling like a fallen hula hoop. Donahue shifted his body so he could push upward against the door, practically kneeling on me.

"Get off," I groaned.

"You get off," he argued. His leg had somehow managed to get stuck under my back.

It took us a few moments before we were able to disentangle ourselves. I accidentally elbowed him in the stomach, and he dug his knees into my ribs trying to climb out. I ended up body pressing him straight up in the air and tossing him out over the side door of The Wheel.

He rolled over and helped me out. I stretched out my arms and cracked my neck. "Let's not tell Vee," I chuckled, thinking about how funny it would have been for someone watching us.

We inspected the damage to The Wheel and discovered the bottom was busted wide open, and the left side was completely destroyed.

"I guess that's why The Wheel wasn't supposed to be driven quite yet," Donahue remarked and began to remove the toolbox that had spilled open.

"Looks like we're walking from here," I sighed, running my finger along the side door and silently saying goodbye.

Donahue and I unloaded the remaining contents, including Amelia —which appeared surprisingly unscathed—from the wreck. Piling as much as we could on top of the control box of Cyril's machine, we hauled it all in the direction of the warehouse. Amelia looked like a futuristic shopping cart.

We walked along, silent and exhausted, and soon my mind wandered to Wren. Where things stood right now, it seemed like it might be impossible to stop her.

Vee's arms were crossed. She'd looked worried when we'd arrived way later than expected. Now, her concern had clearly turned into frustration. "So, you guys almost got zapped by Wren, crashed The Wheel, and then walked a couple hours, pushing Amelia and all that other junk while I waited here thinking something really bad happened?!"

"Yeah," Donahue huffed, walking past her. "I know...I know. We don't have a vehicle now and Wren's furious about her time machine."

"She could have killed you!" Vee ran her olive-toned fingers through her dark hair as she turned to follow us. "I swear, you two are going to be the death of me."

"Relax, Vee, we're okay," I said apologetically and added, "Show us around the warehouse," to change the subject.

We entered a large garage, and a tarp in the back corner caught my attention. I squeezed past some old tires and curiously lifted it up.

"Hey guys! There's an old dirt bike over here!" I announced, coughing as the dust tickled my throat.

The dirt bike looked like it was well settled in its retirement. Rust had taken its toll, and I could see where corrosion had invaded the engine.

Donahue took one look and laughed, "Tolli, even you can't get that thing running."

"It's a start. We need a vehicle."

Vee mumbled, "Not that vehicle."

It was easy to see she was still annoyed at us. She refused to meet my gaze and instead focused on kicking the dirt off her boots.

I ran my fingers over the handlebars, fuzzy dust collecting on my fingertips. "Guys, if we can't fix a bike, how are we gonna build a time machine?" I insisted loudly, pulling the bike up. The seat fell off, and I ignored the amused look Donahue and Vee sent each other. I smiled faintly at the bike, already thinking about what I could salvage from The Wheel to give it a boost.

⇛ 7 YEARS, 3 MONTHS, 26 DAYS, 1 HOUR, and 30 MINUTES to SILEO TERRA

January 31, 2063, 10:30 pm...

Nearly three years after the accident, Wren continued rising to power in Ashborne, adamant the city must adopt her ideals of security. She had revealed herself—unnatural powers, improved robotics, glowing blue eyes, and all. That had been enough to convince the people she was the only one who could take care of them. Or maybe they'd all just been scared. Either way, we could tell her obsessions were escalating as new laws continued to pass in quick succession. We couldn't help the people though; we had to fly under her radar for as long as we could.

Today, we were on a mission to find a rare part we needed to help fuel the boosters on the bottom of the time machine.

I rolled my new and improved dirt bike out of the garage and proudly leapt onto the seat. Donahue followed me outside, shaking his head and smiling as I pulled my messy hair back into a ponytail. I started the engine and zipped forward, spewing mud and sleet behind me. I grinned wildly as I drove a quick lap around the warehouse.

The bike still had a lot of rust on it and wasn't anything fancy to look at, but I was proud of the modifications I had made to it, on top of actually getting it to run. The front jutted out to make the shape more aerodynamic. Beneath the rusted metal was an advanced hydroelectric engine, courtesy of The Wheel. I also had painted a small yellow star on the side, signifying the many late night tests I'd conducted to perfect my pet project.

When I roared up to Donahue, I drove in circles around him a few times. He patiently waited for me to finish.

"You don't have to be a show-off every time you ride this thing," he said as he plopped down behind me.

I pretended to not hear him as I revved the engine, and we took off.

Donahue and I were going to Ashborne to retrieve the part we needed to build a high ignition tank. We planned to build it in the shape of an octagon using titanium, which would help give it enough strength and power to withstand the ignition of the fuel used for propulsion. The tank would also need to be supported by four thick, cone-shaped tubes, also made from titanium. I had traced the part we needed to a house in Ashborne after doing some research at the local library. It belonged to a collector of rare aerospace parts.

Just before we reached our destination, I parked the bike behind a patch of trees and we walked the rest of the way so we wouldn't attract attention. Donahue and I waited until we knew the house was empty before stealthily making our way toward it in the darkness. The snow on the ground softly crunched under our shoes. There was more of it here than at the warehouse.

"Hey, Tolli," Donahue said seriously, "I've been meaning to talk to you about something I was thinking about the other day."

"Oh? What's up?" I asked suspiciously. Most of Donahue's bright ideas included me doing something dangerous or difficult, usually both.

I shone my flashlight on his face. He looked stressed. "Let's get inside first."

As we neared the house, I noticed it had an unusually high chain-link fence around the back.

Donahue sprinted toward the fence and leapt up onto it. It rattled as he climbed over and dropped to the other side. I copied him, but not nearly as smoothly, as his robotics gave him an extra edge. The top of the fence snagged my sweatshirt and I tumbled over, landing in the snow with a thud. He quietly scolded me for falling, and I quietly scolded him for laughing.

I spotted the power box up beside a second-floor window and pointed to it. Donahue read my mind and scaled up the drainpipe to disable the alarm. He gave me a thumbs up, and I quickly picked the lock and entered the small, ornate house.

Donahue joined me, our two flashlights the only source of light in the house. He continued our conversation in the darkness, "Well, we all know there are risks to time travelling, like getting stuck in the past, or even trapped in the threads of time, or somehow not being able to reach Wren when we get there. Anyway, I think—I mean I'm pretty much one hundred percent sure—our current timeline will become unstable if we travel back in time."

"Yeah. You've mentioned that before." I checked the rooms to my left, but they were just bedrooms with lamps and beds and bookshelves and such.

"No." Donahue took a deep breath and continued, "If we fail, if we run out of time, the past, present, and future timelines will collapse. It won't be able to hold if we remove Wren for too long. Then I don't know what would happen."

A shiver crawled up my spine. I nervously joked, "No pressure." Trying to distract myself from his words, I pulled out some books from the shelf in the study we'd just entered. Then, as I grabbed a dusty, dark blue leather book, the shelf swung outward, revealing another alarm system and a locked door. I assumed it led to a basement or a safe, maybe even a safe room.

"Tolli, the world could end," he said gravely. "If we bend a shard of time too far, it will break."

I pondered his words as I disabled the alarm and then picked the lock. I'd been right. The door opened into a passageway with stairs going down to the basement. We made our way into a storage room filled with all kinds of hard-to-find parts we could use. We gathered what we needed into our sacks, along with a few things we didn't necessarily need but looked really cool.

"This has to work," I reminded Donahue, "There's no other way. We have no choice. We'll just have to be quick on our feet."

"Ouch! You just stepped on me!"

"Shh! Sorry."

6 YEARS, 9 MONTHS, 5 HOURS, and 24 MINUTES to SILEO TERRA

August 27, 2063, 6:36 pm...

"**P**ass me that pencil, Vee." Donahue was hunched over the designs we had taken from Wren's room.

We had finally begun construction on the new machine, but we'd had to make a couple big changes from Wren's original plan. It had taken us months to put together a new blueprint incorporating Amelia and even longer to find all the basic parts we needed to begin. We'd had to examine it to figure out how it worked and how we could connect it to the new Tempus. Once we'd had a good idea of how everything should be put together, we'd finally started building.

Wren had continued to gain power in Ashborne, and people had accepted her ideas of security, mostly in fear, but the three of us knew Wren. We knew what she had been through and that she wasn't mentally stable. We had concluded time travel was the only answer to our problems as Wren's obsession with control and power and security had pushed her to the brink of insanity. Her personal power and abilities had also grown, reducing the probability of anyone being able to stop her.

Vee bit down on an apple and tossed him the pencil. Donahue caught it and started sketching on a scrap piece of paper. "So, this is the main part that will deviate from Wren's design. We'll attach Cyril's disc to the top of Tempus III, and the disc will open the threads of time." He drew the clawed disc from Amelia on top of a rough rectangular prism.

"And we're definitely getting rid of that awful noise Amelia makes," Vee announced firmly. "There's no way we're time travelling that way."

Remembering the ear-splitting ring, I shivered and joked, "Should have been called 'Screams of Amelia.'"

Donahue laughed and assured us, "Don't worry, we'll make Amelia whisper. Then, everything else pretty much stays the same as before but on a slightly larger scale to fit us all."

Us. We were the last. All that remained of DAWN. A sudden pang of grief filled my heart as I remembered the dead faces of DAWN agents staring blankly into nothingness. They had died when Wren had tried to start her time machine. She had merged with the orb, causing a huge time storm and creating enough blue lightning to fill the entire facility. It had killed everyone inside. Vee and I had been away on a mission to get Wren help after she had erased her memory, so we hadn't been there to witness it like Donahue had been. We had only witnessed the aftermath, and it had been gruesome.

"Do you guys still see their faces in your dreams?" I asked, gazing up at the bare ceiling. They knew who I was talking about.

Donahue mumbled, "Rob Mallick."

"Silvia Mercier. Adeline Jessie," Vee added.

They added a few more names to the list of dead friends, and then we all grew silent.

"How will the time machine be propelled into the time dimension?" Vee inquired, hastily changing the subject.

"I'm working on constructing the engine and booster on the bottom. That should provide it with enough thrust," I replied and absentmindedly chewed on the eraser of my pencil.

"So, we're ditching the lightning trigger entirely," Vee stated rather than asked.

Donahue explained, "It's too dangerous. We have Amelia, which hypothetically can do the same thing but in a different way."

"What do you mean?"

"I think," he said, putting his fist under his chin, "that's what it was doing when we first interacted with it, when Cyril first turned it on. It was holding open a portal to the dimension containing the threads of time. It's far more effective than a lightning trigger, trust me."

Amelia sat in the corner of the workroom we had set up in the main part of the warehouse. I walked over to retrieve it and rolled it back to Donahue and Vee. I bent down to study the metal claws. "If we could disconnect the disc, we wouldn't need the control box." I fetched a pocket-knife and sliced a thin line through the rubber base. Vee and Donahue watched as I examined the nest of wires and the liquid fuel encased inside.

"This is going to take a long, long time."

"That's okay. We'll have all the time in the world when we finish the time machine," Vee smiled.

Donahue looked through some of Wren's blueprints and muttered, "It sure will be nice to see the old Wren again."

Vee and I exchanged glances. "You do realize she won't know any of us, right?"

Donahue smiled wearily. "Don't worry, I can barely remember what she was like either."

I walked over to his side and said, "Not crazy, that's for sure."

"No," he denied, "she was always a little crazy." He playfully punched me in the shoulder clearly not wanting to think about her anymore. "Why don't you go make us something to eat, Chef Tolli?"

I gave him a quick salute and walked away. I knew we didn't have much for food because it had been a while since our last grocery run, but I was a genius at making delicious meals with whatever I could find. If Donahue or Vee were in charge of the cooking, we would have starved to death a long time ago. I strolled to the old lunchroom where I kept all the supplies. The problem with keeping it stocked was that we could only get as much as we could carry back from Ashborne on the bike. Truth be told, though, I didn't mind all the trips because it was still the best way to be discreet, and we weren't exactly law-abiding citizens when it came to picking up supplies and groceries.

I looked up at the old clock on the wall. Tick, tock. Tick, tock. Tick, tock. It would keep counting until we could set things back on the right course.

≋ 4 YEARS, 10 MONTHS, 22 DAYS, 7 HOURS, and 20 MINUTES to SILEO TERRA

July 5, 2065, 4:40 pm...

The construction of the bubble shield was both a wonder and a curse. I hadn't been trapped on the inside of it, thankfully, but I'd kept watch as the huge generator had been built on the outskirts of Ashborne. The brilliant pink and purple force field leapt back and forth over the city like sheet lightning. If the whole horrible idea hadn't been something thought up and controlled by Wren, it would have been a beautiful sight.

Wren had forced her ideas of utopia onto the people of Ashborne for the last four years. Some people were convinced her plans were good and necessary, and others felt they didn't have a choice. Her goal was to eliminate all threats—whether real or perceived—to the city, in part by enforcing a strong security system, which included the bubble shield. Anything that touched it would die immediately. Wren was right; it could protect the city, but what Wren failed to notice, or didn't care about, was that it also imprisoned the city.

I was perched on the roof of the warehouse, staring at the bright shield, which was now permanently on. Vee and Donahue lounged on either side of me. We were taking a much-needed break from working on Tempus III.

"What are we going to do now?" Vee sighed in frustration.

The construction of the generator had taken place over three weeks, but now it was complete. Wren had designed it and then hired—or forced, we really didn't know—people to build it for her.

Vee's fists were clenched at her sides, and I suspected she was going to look for something to punch soon.

I put my hands up defensively and said, "I know you're mad, Vee, but before you start kicking and karate chopping things, I just want to remind you that Donahue and I are off limits." She glared at me and I shifted closer to Donahue. Vee reached out and punched me in the shoulder. "Ouch."

"You were asking for it," she mumbled, but I detected a hint of a smile.

I was about to tease her further, but Donahue intercepted me. "Guys." He looked serious. "I don't think we can go much longer without a real vehicle." He cautiously glanced at me as my smile disappeared and I crossed my arms. He continued, "We'll have to travel further for supplies if we can't get into Ashborne. The bike can only hold so much."

Vee looked back and forth between us, confusion on her face.

25 YEARS, 10 MONTHS, 1 DAY, 11 HOURS, and 29 MINUTES to SILEO TERRA

July 26, 2044, 1:31 pm...

"Scoot over, Trevy!" Ace nudged me aside and plopped down beside me on the concrete floor of the garage.

It was hot out today, so Ace and I had decided to cool off inside. I had snuck a pack of chalk in so we could sketch on the concrete. At six years old, I had just discovered chalk, and I drew on anything and everything. I loved it because I could just wipe it off and start all over again. It drove my mom crazy when I drew race cars on the walls.

I took a white piece of chalk and drew a stick person with a baseball cap and a wrench. "This is Dad." *It looks a lot like him*, I thought to myself proudly after I added the recognizable blue eyes and curly blonde hair.

Ace giggled and showed me his chalk drawing of an upside-down top hat with a white blob jumping out of it.

"What's that?" I asked, pointing to the blob and wiping my blonde hair out of my face with my other hand.

"That's a rabbit, duh. And you have chalk on your forehead," he laughed.

I shrugged. Next, I drew Mom. She had brown eyes and thick wavy hair that seemed to change colour every week. "What colour is Mom's hair right now?"

"Black, red—no—purple," Ace replied, handing me a stick of purple chalk.

I furrowed my brow. "What's her real hair colour?"

"I...um...don't know. Rainbow?"

"Rainbow it is," I concluded and grabbed a handful of chalk to fill in Mom's hair. I also gave her a screwdriver—because she liked to work alongside my dad in the garage—and a black phone since she was constantly talking on it.

Suddenly, we heard voices and footsteps on the other side of the garage. Ace motioned for me to go out through the door to our left, but it was too late. The grownups had spotted us. Both Mom and Dad wore faded blue overalls, and Mom's red bandana partially hid short brown hair with ends tinged orange and yellow. Her face was covered in make-up, which meant bright red lipstick and dark eye shadow. Dad was smeared with dirt and grease, which wasn't surprising since that was his normal look.

Next to my parents was a man I had never seen before. He looked scary in his ripped jeans and tight tank top that showed tattoos crawling up his muscular arms and neck. A scruffy beard hung from his face, and his expression remained in a permanent scowl.

Dad waved a hand at us, "Oh, these are my sons, Trevor and Aaron."

"Sweethearts, can you go play somewhere else?" Mom asked and pointed to the door we were standing beside. "Mommy and Daddy are working in here today."

They were both mechanics and worked in the garage almost every day. They seemed to love their work, and secretly, I think they hoped Ace and I would become mechanics too. Today, they had a huge white truck they were going to paint in the garage, judging from the cans of black automotive paint stacked up beside it.

I looked at Ace and nodded, and we walked out without another word. I often wondered about the strange people that came to visit Mom and Dad in the garage, so I strained to catch a few words on the way out.

"How old are they?" a deep voice asked suspiciously.

"Six and ten. They're fine, man. They don't know anything."

⇛ 4 YEARS, 10 MONTHS, and 21 DAYS to SILEO TERRA

July 7, 2065, 12:00 am...

Donahue knew my family history, so when we had discussed needing a vehicle, he had delicately offered to take care of finding one himself. I had adamantly dismissed that idea, even though I had made a promise to myself a long time ago that I would never end up like my parents or Ace, that I would control my life and the direction it took. My parents had been so proud of Ace when he had decided to take over their business, but that was the day I had walked away. The last time I had even talked to my dad on the phone was when I'd gotten accepted into DAWN. He'd hung up immediately upon hearing the news.

In the end, Donahue and Vee had decided to revisit the conversation later in the week.

After a few sleepless hours, I got out of bed and paced back and forth, my mind wracked with internal turmoil. I kicked the wall in frustration and immediately regretted it as I staggered back and held my throbbing toe. Thankfully, I caught myself before falling on Donahue's sleeping body. I looked down at him, surprised he was still fast asleep as he lay on the cold ground with a blanket covering half of his body, a screwdriver next to his limp hand. We had decided to share a room while Vee claimed her own room down the hall. I looked around our room; the mess came mostly from kicking our junk into the corners and never moving anything unless we had to.

I had sworn to myself that I would never steal a car again, and there aren't many things more discouraging than breaking a promise to yourself. My choices were the only things I had ever had control over in my life. Now I was faced with a difficult one. On the one hand, I could refuse to do this for the team—I mean, we hadn't even come to a decision on who would steal the car yet—but on the other hand, I would never be able to live with myself if I just let Donahue and Vee do it and they got caught. It made way more sense for a former car thief to steal a car.

I sighed and asked myself, "Yes or no? You have to choose."

I plopped down on my old ripped mattress, which creaked loudly, and I wiped the sweat from my brow. I had made up my mind. The hard part had been deciding what to do; the easy part was actually doing it. I knew exactly how to steal a car.

First, I filled my backpack with supplies. I stopped to rub the worn leather on the small kit my dad had given me as a kid. As eager as I'd been to leave my family behind, I had never been able to bring myself to throw this kit away. I wrote a short note on a scrap piece of paper and set it on my empty pillow before sneaking out of the room. The quick scribbles read, "Going 2 Willowdale, b back soon w/car—T." Carefully, I made my way through the warehouse, up the stairs, and out the front door, inadvertently adding to the chips in the old, white, pockmarked frame.

I took a deep breath of the cool, brisk air and stepped out into the darkness. Immediately, I started having second thoughts and began pacing again in front of the building while dragging my fingers through my blonde locks. This whole situation brought back a lot of bad memories.

I stopped, bit down on my lip, and stared into the pitch-black night. When my eyes adjusted to the darkness, I gazed at the twinkling stars and the sliver of moon peeking out from behind the clouds.

I gave myself a pep talk out loud. "I'm doing this to save the fate of humanity. If I don't do this, my friends and I don't survive. If we don't survive, we can't fix anything."

So, was I going to go through with this?

I clicked on the small flashlight in my hand and started jogging.

I didn't have a choice.

I collapsed when I reached the outskirts of Willowdale and rested for a moment after the long jog. It had taken me hours to get here. The field of grass was so soft and inviting I could feel my eyes beginning to droop. I willed my body back on track; I could sleep once I completed my mission. I munched on a protein bar as I rubbed the exhaustion from my eyes and stood back up.

With its quaint neighbourhoods and small family-run businesses, this city was small compared to Ashborne. My cousin, Gage, and his family had lived here once, so I had spent a lot of time hanging around here when I was young. Willowdale's worn facades betrayed its age compared to Ashborne. Some buildings were completely dilapidated while newer ones were small and simple by design but still in good condition. I looked around and wondered whether Wren's plans included just expanding the shield over all the nearby cities or building individual generators around all the cities in the world. Her lust for power and control would most certainly not stay in Ashborne.

It was important to choose my vehicle carefully. I stayed in the shadows as I wandered through the back streets looking for the perfect target. Along with the darkness, the natural fogginess of early morning was a great asset in keeping me hidden, but I knew this would be temporary. I had to move quickly before the sun woke up. I wanted something that wouldn't be missed, and with some luck, wouldn't even be looked for. That meant I needed to find something that wasn't the lone vehicle outside a home or anything worth a lot of money. Also, it needed enough room to easily fit the three of us plus any supplies we were carrying.

It didn't take long before I found what I was looking for. My target was an old pickup truck that probably had equal parts rust to paint, and it was parked in a back alley in the industrial part of the city. Opposite the alley was the back of a closed grocery store with a sign above the door that read, "In a Pickle." I thought that was fitting as I would definitely be in a pickle if I got caught.

A large storage shed beside the truck helped shield me from prying eyes. The setting seemed too perfect, and I could feel my mind spinning, knowing what I was about to do, but the knot in my stomach confirmed I needed to get moving. The bad memories were going to eat away at me until I had completed the job.

When I was sure no one was nearby and it was just light enough to see what I was doing, I strolled up to the vehicle and pulled on the handle. It was locked. I sighed and pulled out my kit. I stared at it for a moment, remembering how often I had used it as a teenager. It felt surreal as my childhood skills returned to me in a rush, and before I knew it, I was inside the truck.

I slipped on the gloves from my backpack so I wouldn't burn my hands on the wires and ducked under the dash to locate the three screws under the steering wheel. I was able to unscrew them all with ease and carefully remove the plastic cover. This revealed a ton of wiring, and for a moment, I panicked, trying to recollect what I'd learned as a teenager. I took a deep breath and counted to three. No movement, no noise. I was fine.

"There are three bundles, Trevy. You're looking for the steering column one."

I hated that I had to recall my brother showing me how to hotwire a car, but I still whispered a quiet thanks to Ace.

I separated two red wires and one yellow wire from the steering column bundle and grabbed my pocketknife so I could cut off their protective plastic. After I frayed the ends, I twisted the two red ones around each other with the pliers, causing the dashboard to light up.

"Lightly touch the starter wire to those ones and voila!"

I grabbed the yellow wire and cautiously touched it to the entangled red wires. The truck started, and I jumped into the driver's seat, turned the steering wheel sharply, and stomped on the gas pedal, speeding away.

I caught myself grinning in the rear-view mirror, which immediately made me feel guilty. I wanted to punch myself in the face.

"Trevy, now you're a car thief, just like us!"

1 DAY, 11 HOURS, and 30 MINUTES to SILEO TERRA

May 26, 2070, 12:30 pm...

It felt surreal as Donahue exclaimed, "Tempus III is finished!"

"Tempus III is finished," I echoed. "Honestly, I knew we'd be able to do it," I lied happily.

He met my gaze and smirked, "Me too."

"Do you like how I decorated it?" I asked as we walked up to the door.

Vee joined us and huffed, "It's stark white, and there's nothing in it except the basics."

Finally, after over a decade of Wren's destruction, Tempus III stood tall, with a few key amendments from the original. Donahue had installed Cyril's technology on it, and the disc was now perched on top of the silver, rectangular-shaped time machine. There were now larger rectangular windows on each side in contrast to Wren's round windows, and it had boosters on the bottom and sides to help it navigate through the threads of time. The interior had a similar control desk and screens to Tempus II but also had four seats: one for each of us, including our special passenger. I hoped the biggest change we'd made was that it would actually work.

"I guess I'm a minimalist." I shrugged with a grin.

"Says the guy who doesn't throw anything away," Vee teased, but then her tone shifted, "We're really messing with time, huh?" I could hear the tension in her voice. Vee sounded nervous and anxious, but there was a hint of excitement too. She sounded like what we were all feeling.

Donahue stepped forward. "Okay, guys, let's go over the plan one last time. Vee will pilot Tempus III, navigating us through the dimension that holds the threads of time. When Tempus III attaches us to the correct thread, we'll travel backward to reach past Wren by creating a shard of time, or station, to stop at. When we get there, I'll go out and grab her. You guys stay put. When we have her, the four of us will travel back here to the present, causing her timeline to freeze for an undetermined length of time—hopefully long enough to complete the mission. When we get back here, she'll be disoriented and confused, so we can't push her, but we must present our plan to her clearly and persuasively since we're asking her to help us fight against…well, herself."

Donahue paused to look at us and then started pacing as he continued, "Once we convince her to join us, we'll move onto the next stage, where we bring Wren and her future self face to face in her headquarters. Oh, and no one can see any of this. They can't see us grab her, and they can't see us sending her back. If future Wren figures out any of this, she'll stop us immediately. Hopefully, we can avoid violence. I think past Wren will be able to talk to future Wren and reason with her. By altering Wren's fate, the timeline will have to change. If we succeed, this timeline will collapse and a new one will take its place." He paused to let the enormity of our mission sink in. "Sound good?"

I looked him dead in the eye. "I got all that…but I don't think anyone else did." I gestured toward Vee with my head, and she responded by rolling her eyes. I continued, "So, to clarify, can you repeat the whole thing over again?"

Donahue smiled faintly and playfully responded, "We get Wren from the past and save the future."

"This could be a huge mistake," Vee muttered, but she followed us into the time machine anyway.

This was it. This was our chance to do it all over again. It was a chance to right Wren's wrongs.

We closed the time machine's hatch and looked at the four seats inside. Three sat in a half circle in the centre, and one was placed at the touch-screen control desk. Vee went straight to her seat at the control desk, but Donahue and I leaned against the small ledges that jutted out from the inner walls, unable—or unwilling—to sit down right away. He crossed his arms and glared straight ahead, obviously battling mixed emotions about seeing Wren again.

Vee touched a few buttons on the screen, and taking a deep breath, I sat down in one of the centre chairs. Humming and whirring noises from outside the time machine meant it was ready to go. Then, like a tiny quake, everything around began to shake, and the intensity of the roar gave way to the mighty rumbles of a thunderstorm. Hopefully grabbing Wren from the past would be easy.

≡ PART FIVE ≡
WREN DERECHO

May 26, 2070, 10:01 pm...

"**C**ome on, Wren, I want to show you something." That was Alex's only answer to all the questions I was peppering him with. He turned around to leave. I hesitated for a second but decided I didn't want to be left alone in this strange future world just yet.

"Alex? Wait up!" I called after him.

If anyone was going to give me a good explanation, I was sure it would be Alex. My footsteps pounded behind him as I worked to keep up with his long strides. I suddenly stopped in my tracks, debating whether I wanted to see what he was going to show me. He slowed down and looked back at me.

"Wren? You okay?"

I asked suspiciously, "How can I trust you?"

He sighed and shook his head. "I can't make you trust me. I can't make you do anything. All I'm asking you to do is see for yourself and give me a chance to explain."

Something in my gut told me it might be okay to trust these people. After all, Uncle William had wanted me to meet Alex before he had died. I decided to follow him out the door, telling myself it didn't mean I had to agree to anything.

He led me outside, where the sun was now a sliver on the horizon, its golden hue bleeding into the sky. To my surprise, we circled around to the back where oak trees had grown above the roof, stretching their leaves and branches out against the building. Alex secured one foot to the side of the building and the other against a tree. Gracefully, he climbed up to the roof. I mirrored his movements, making it up faster than he had.

"It's beautiful up here," I remarked when I reached the top and sat beside him.

Alex was silent for a few seconds and then pointed and whispered, "Look." My eyes followed his finger, and I was stunned at the pinky purple dome in the distance, crackling with an electric glow. It appeared to be surrounding blurry structures.

"Ashborne?" I guessed.

"Yes. It was the first of its kind, and soon there will be other cities like it. We've discovered more generators are being built. No one goes in, and no one comes out without Wren's permission." Alex met my gaze, the wind blowing his black hair into his eyes. "But we have a plan that could save our future...and also save you."

"And that is...?" My voice trailed off; I was pretty sure I wouldn't like his explanation.

"We'll take you to Ashborne to confront your future self. You'll do whatever you must to defeat her. Best case scenario, you reason with her. Get her to see things from a different viewpoint. You're the only one that knows at least a part of what's in her head. She might listen to you. After all, you're the same person. You might be able to understand her." A sad look momentarily crossed his face. "Then we'll take you back in Tempus III—to your present—before the timeline collapses. All of this," he waved his arm and then pushed himself up, "is about you, Wren."

"Tempus III?" I felt a little flattered.

"It's still a really good name for a time machine."

I wasn't sure I saw any other choice. They kept telling me if I didn't choose to defeat myself, future me would destroy the world with her— my—need for control and security. If I did nothing, time would take us all: all our freedom, all our desire, all our ambition, everything that made us human. Everything felt out of my control all of a sudden.

I stood up and started pacing back and forth on the roof. I was confused and frustrated, and I didn't want to be forced to do anything.

A nagging in my brain pulled at me, a voice emerging from the depths of my thoughts.

"It won't work. Your future self is too powerful. You have no control over what happens. And for all you know, he could be feeding you lies," it hissed.

"Wren?" Alex's voice interrupted my thoughts. "If this is too overwhelming, we can talk more tomorrow." I sat back down beside him. He sighed. "We guessed it would be hard for you to take in all this information."

"It's not like all of this is your fault. You haven't done anything wrong. You don't have to help them."

I shook my head to rid myself of the taunting voice. Was I going crazy?

"There is something you should know, though. It might be tough to hear, but you should know," Alex said, so quietly I hardly heard him.

Wrapping my arms around my knees, I looked over at him. I was pretty sure I didn't want to hear this, but now that he'd said it, I had to know. "What?"

"A long time ago—or I guess a short time in the future for you—something upset you and you accidentally hurt me. You felt so terrible you just couldn't live with it, so you found a way to erase your memory. Without your memories, you had nothing to keep you grounded. You decided to start up Tempus II, but instead of travelling through time, the orb merged itself with you. When that happened, it created a time storm and generated an electrical explosion in the building...it killed everyone...including Rob."

The air left my lungs. I felt like I'd been punched in the gut. I, she, we did that. We had killed Rob. Rob, the man who had only ever wanted the best for me. Rob, the only person I'd felt I could trust. I whispered, through teary eyes, "I'm a horrible person."

Alex squeezed his eyes shut and sighed, "My mama used to tell me this: 'It's important not to let the bad people and negative experiences keep you from seeing the good in those around you—the most undesirable of people can find redemption. Sometimes people can make bad decisions and mistakes in life that lead them down the wrong path, but don't give up on them too soon. You need to give them a chance.' We're giving you that chance now, Wren."

I dropped my head onto my arms and looked at the floor. What was I going to become if I did nothing? I couldn't just sit back and let myself turn into this monster. I would hurt even more innocent people. Sadly, part of me wasn't surprised to hear that my future self was now obsessed with control, even more than I currently was.

Alex took a deep breath and tried again, "Wren, this is your one chance to set things right. This is where you redeem yourself in this timeline."

"Okay," I finally said, "I'm in." I exhaled loudly. Why had I been arguing over this?

Alex stood and extended a strong calloused hand to help me up. I took it. "If you're ready, let's get into the details of the plan. We don't have to wait until tomorrow."

1 DAY and 1 MINUTE to SILEO TERRA

May 26, 2070, 11:59 pm...

N ow the voice inside my head was constant and I could no longer ignore it. It tortured me as I lay on my bed unable to close my eyes.
"Can't you see? There's no way to know for sure if all your efforts will do anything. You can't win this fight."

I rubbed my temples, willing the voice to go away. I tossed and turned on my mattress, unable to find a comfortable position.

"Who are you?" I questioned through clenched teeth.

"I am you, and you are me."

"No," I muttered under my breath.

I looked over at Cass, but she was fast asleep, curled up in a sleeping bag on the floor. I fixed my gaze up at the ceiling. My eyelids were heavy from exhaustion but couldn't close as the voice continued relentlessly. I was going to face myself tomorrow, and the voice was becoming insistent on discouraging me.

Frustrated, I dragged myself off the old mattress I was lying on while holding the orb ahead of me to light the way. I was careful not to wake Cass.

"You can't get away that easily."

I stumbled out of the room and found my way to the main area downstairs. It seemed foolish to try to get away from something inside my head, but I tried anyway. My breathing shallowed, and I felt a heavy weight against my chest. I stopped walking and rubbed my eyes with my hand, entangling the messy red strands of my hair in my metal fingers.

"Get out," I demanded. I accidentally bumped into a nearby table, knocking over some papers and causing the metal legs to scrape against the ground.

"I am a part of you. I am you."

"Wren?"

I spun around, my eyes wide. That was a different voice. Alex shuffled in. His hair was messy, and there were dark shadows under his sleepy eyes. "What are you doing?" he asked wearily.

"We are one and the same."

"Um…uh…nothing," I stuttered.

Immediately, my heart rate skyrocketed, and I felt like I was engulfed in a sea of confusion and darkness that threatened to drown me.

"Breathe, breathe, breathe," I pleaded in my head. But I couldn't, I couldn't breathe! My pulse throbbed in my ears and sweat collected across my forehead. What was happening to me?

I reached out to grab a small stool next to me, but it couldn't hold my weight and it tipped over. The loud clatter made me flinch, and I stuttered, "I knocked it—sorry—I'm…over."

I trembled as the room started spinning and the ground became unstable. I tried to keep my balance by clenching my fists, but my legs gave out and my vision turned black.

When I regained consciousness a few moments later, I was propped up against the wall, breathing heavily. Alex knelt beside me with his hand on my shoulder and a look of concern in his eyes. My head was throbbing as I slid against the wall and leaned against his outstretched arm.

"You collapsed," he explained, and then added, "You're not okay, Wren. What's going on?"

"Have you had enough?" the voice inside my head mocked, laughing.

I winced but stayed silent as my pulse picked up again.

Alex straightened me up and sat down right in front of me so he could maintain eye contact. There was almost no light in the room, but I could see the light from the orb I still clutched in my fist reflecting in his eyes. His pupils looked like deep pools of black obsidian, and for a moment I couldn't look away.

"What's the matter? Did you have a panic attack?" he questioned gently.

"No, it was nothing," I repeated.

"*Liar.*"

I blurted out, "What?! What did you call me?" My cheeks grew hot with a sudden burst of fury that quickly shifted into embarrassment when I saw the confusion and concern wash over Alex's face. I rolled away from him to lie on the ground and curled up into the fetal position, focusing on my breathing. Inhale, exhale.

"I'm not crazy," I whispered.

"Wren, look at me." I slowly turned my head and looked up at his dark hazel eyes. "Breathe. Everything's going to be okay."

I finally admitted, "She's gotten into my head, Donna." I was on the brink of tears.

Alex responded softly, "I know you're feeling overwhelmed. And frustrated. Angry probably. And sad. I just want you to know you're not alone. I'll listen to you."

"You forgot scared," I added quietly.

"She can't see you right now. The three of us will protect you," Alex replied calmly.

"Why do I have to do this alone? Why do I have to talk to her?"

"Wren, no one is beyond redemption. If anyone could get through to her, it would be you." He waited for my reply, but I didn't say anything, so he changed the subject. "So, you're still going to call me Donna?" He grinned softly, his smile immediately making me feel calmer. I still didn't say anything, but I could feel the tension ease from my body. "Trust me, everything's going to be okay," he assured me.

His gaze moved up to the ceiling as the pitter-patter of rain grew louder. "There's a storm brewing," he muttered.

"Want to know something disturbing?" I asked, thankful for something else to talk about. I waved my hand in the air. "A derecho is a widespread, long-lived, straight-line windstorm with wind so powerful the group of severe thunderstorms formed is unstoppable."

"That is a little concerning," Alex admitted gingerly.

Everything was so confusing and crazy, and the thought of facing my future self seemed terrifying and unrealistic at the same time; however, if everything went according to plan, I would see myself tomorrow. The overwhelming emotions crashed over me like giant waves churning in my mind, threatening to crush my very soul. What had future me done to these people?

"I am a horrible person," I repeated and felt my breathing start to shorten again. "I wish I could forget my past and this future…it's just…"

"No, don't forget. Don't ever forget," Alex interjected urgently. "That's what your future self did. She erased her memory when things became too hard for her. If you forget, you can't recall the memories that can keep you going when things are hard," Alex answered calmly while putting his hand over mine. I could feel the gentle warmth from his hand, and for a moment, my heart fluttered as he wiped my tears away with his other hand. "Your name fits you well: you are strong, you stand up and fight for what you believe in, and you too will be unstoppable," he finished.

I was amused at the confidence in his voice. "How do you know how to make me feel better?"

He scooted closer to sit beside me, leaned his head against the wall, and closed his eyes. "We were quite close a long time ago." I slowly sat up and looked at him.

"Oh yeah? Well, then, what's my favourite colour?" I asked jokingly.

"Trick question. You told me it was the colour of space."

I chuckled and continued, "What's my middle name?"

"That's easy, Amber," Alex responded. "It was your mother's name."

I thought of my mother. I remembered how her freckles softened her kind smile and my eyes watered.

Alex was smiling warmly now, and his eyes, reflecting what little light they could, looked distant, like his mind was far away reminiscing about a happier time. I watched as his look of happiness gave way to a look of pain, and I decided maybe it was time to stop talking.

I stifled a yawn. "If it's okay, I'm just going to sleep here." I folded my hands under my head as I curled up on the ground again. Alex stood up and walked away but soon returned with a thick blanket to cover me with.

Even though I didn't want to be alone, I suggested, "You should go back to bed, Alex."

"Don't worry about me." He grabbed a couple of tools from his toolbox and headed over to the time machine. "Sweet dreams."

I could hear him tinkering away and was thankful for it. The noise meant he was close by. I drifted off to sleep feeling safe and happy for the first time in as long as I could remember.

14 HOURS and 41 MINUTES to SILEO TERRA

May 27, 2070, 9:19 am...

I tossed aside the dirty beige blanket that had kept me warm all night. My hair was a tangled mess, and my muscles were sore from sleeping on the hard floor. I had drifted in and out of consciousness after I'd first fallen asleep listening to Alex's tinkering, hearing the voice in my dreams, haunting me. I looked around and saw that Alex was gone.

I made my way to the lunchroom to search for something to eat and couldn't help but notice the empty cabinets as I sifted through them. I settled for a box of dry flaky cereal. I stuck my metallic hand in and grabbed a handful to munch on as I walked over to a chair and sat down.

The lights flickered twice, and I felt a strange pulse of energy. I pulled the orb out of my pocket and swore it looked like a beating heart for a few seconds.

Cass's shouts from the main room reached me a few seconds before she did. She peeked in and nodded. "Oh, there you are. Hey, I'm sorry about yesterday. Are we good?"

I nodded my head gratefully.

"Okay, come look at this," she spoke in a serious tone.

I dropped the box of cereal and followed her back to the large workroom where Tempus III stood.

Cass whispered, "We're almost set, but the weirdest thing happened: the time machine started up on its own."

I stared at the metal box with its windows and singular door. Boosters were attached to the bottom, and I noticed the lightning trigger had been replaced with a different contraption. I walked closer to get a better look at it. My mind started spinning as I wondered how it worked. The lights suddenly switched on, and the time machine rose a few inches before returning to the ground with a loud thud.

"It's what Alex was talking about: the timeline is straining to sustain itself," I gasped. Alex had mentioned that last night. I made the timeline unstable by being here. That's why we needed to hurry.

"We need to get this done." Her gray eyes looked worried.

Nodding, I tried to push away the fear growing in the pit of my stomach. I needed to fulfill the mission they had given me. I had to reason with, overcome, or eliminate my future self to save the world from enslavement.

"Or you could help me. You are just delaying the inevitable."

Startled, I dropped the orb and scrambled to pick it up and shove it back into my pocket.

"This is my mess, and I need to fix my mistakes," I said determinedly.

Cass placed an olive-toned hand on my metal one and gave it a squeeze. "I know this wasn't fair of us to ask," she sighed. "Thank you for helping us. I always believed in you, even when we were children. You'll figure it out. I know you will. You always do."

Cass had said this to me once before, ages ago, in what seemed like another world. I looked into her eyes and tried to believe her. There was no going back now. There was no second guessing. There was no giving up.

"That's easier said than done."

11 HOURS and 13 MINUTES to SILEO TERRA

May 27, 2070, 12:47 pm...

This was the plan: we would find a way into her headquarters tonight, I would face myself, and all that mattered after that was that I got out of this timeline. It was all about me.

As soon as the final preparations were complete, the four of us would drive to Ashborne and get through the force field. The boys had rigged up a shield disabler: a large black and silver device that curved into a wide upside-down "U" shape that reminded me of a melon rind. Once it was attached to the bed and part of the roof of the truck, it would allow us to drive through the shield undetected. The curved edges would send out signals to divert the shield's rays for a few seconds, creating a safe passage for our truck to pass through. That was the easy part. Getting to Wren was the difficult part. Confronting Wren was the terrifying part.

As I ran through the plan in my head, I stared at the clock in the supply room. While it told me it was lunch time, I was anything but hungry. I wasn't ready for what was to come.

Alex and Tolli were making last minute adjustments to the shield disabler and attaching it to their vehicle, so I'd been sent in here to grab Alex's backpack and a few extra things he thought we would need. It looked like random things had been thrown everywhere in here: clothes, rusty tools, papers, and even empty grocery bags and garbage. As I looked around, I kept getting distracted by the clock.

Tick, tock. Tick, tock. I couldn't tear my gaze from it. Tick, tock. Tick, tock. It was keeping track of time, something every person relied on for order and precision. Tick, tock. Tick, tock. Except we had found a way around it. Suddenly, the clock stopped. Its hands froze and the lights flickered twice before the clock started again.

Cass rushed into the room. "Are you okay, Wren? The lights are being weird again."

"I'm fine," I replied, without pulling my gaze from the clock. *"Are you?"*

I grabbed a pair of pliers and a screwdriver and added them to the rest of the stuff in Alex's large backpack.

Cass squinted her eyes as she looked up at the wall. When she realized what time it was, her gray eyes widened. "We don't have much time. Donahue's pretty sure the timeline will collapse today. I better go give those guys a hand."

I panicked for a second and dug my hand into my pocket. I sighed with relief as I pulled out the orb. It was safe and sound.

"I'll never leave you."

Cass eyed me suspiciously. "Don't get too attached to it," she warned.

8 HOURS and 45 MINUTES to SILEO TERRA

May 27, 2070, 3:15 pm...

I stared at the glowing orb. It was beautiful. I held it out and ran my finger over the smooth surface. It was hard to believe this stunning object was the source of all my troubles.

"Are you sure it's not your new friends causing all the trouble?"

Cass peeked in again and her voice broke my trance.

"Wren, the guys are almost finished attaching the shield disabler to the truck. Are you ready to go?"

I nodded and followed her into the garage, where the device was sitting on the truck bed with a bundle of rope resting on top of it. It felt like days had passed while I'd been busy arguing with the orb, but it had only been a few hours. Still, it had taken them a long time to get that thing on the truck.

Alex and Tolli were arguing over how to triple-secure the disabler since they needed to make sure it wouldn't fall off. They had already screwed the shield disabler to a base attached to the bed, the frame, and the roof of the truck, and reinforced that with scrap metal, but they weren't taking any chances.

"Do you even know how to tie a knot?" Tolli squinted his eyes accusingly.

"Oh yeah, remember all that time I spent sailing the high seas?" Alex fired back sarcastically.

Cass shoved them both aside and grabbed a fistful of rope. "I'll do the tying!"

The boys looked relieved as Cass gave sharp orders to the rest of us. We shifted the device tightly in place and weaved the rope back and forth while Cass tied tight knots. When we finished, she dusted off her hands and quipped, "That wasn't too hard, was it?"

Her question was met with silence and eye rolling.

Cass clapped her hands together and answered her own question, "Yup, it's good," as she made her way to the driver's seat.

Alex slung the backpack I'd brought in over his shoulder, and we scrambled to the truck. Its dark brown paint was old and chipped, and I silently wondered if it could even get us where we needed to go, let alone make it back. I flung the door open with a nervous energy that almost took the hinges off.

Alex's backpack collided with my elbow as he threw it in beside me and jumped in before slamming the door shut.

Sunlight flooded in as Tolli opened the garage door. Cass started the truck, and we zoomed outside before skidding to a stop to let Tolli in after he'd closed the garage door behind us. Cass playfully swatted Tolli's head when he threw himself into the passenger seat and bumped against her. It was amazing how Tolli could still lighten the mood even when faced with as daunting a task as we had. I shifted in my torn, fabric-lined seat and looked out the back window as we drove away. As the warehouse shrunk from my view, I thought about how I would miss this place and these three individuals. Within a few minutes, the overgrowth of vegetation hid most of the warehouse from view, and the massive oaks sheltered the building with their bright leaves.

I clutched the orb in my fist and felt my anxiety escalate during the twenty-minute ride to Ashborne.

"You know they won't make it. It always ends up with you being alone. Join me. Fulfill your destiny."

I shivered so hard my teeth chattered even though I wasn't cold. It was only a matter of time before I came face to face with the person I dreaded most: myself.

"We can't go near the checkpoints on the north and south side of the city. I think the east side will do," Alex instructed Cass.

We arrived at the outskirts of the city, and Tolli got out to activate the shield disabler. Once he was back in the truck, Vee inched us forward as the crackle of lightning threatened to devour our vehicle. The bright flashes of light tinged with purple left me in a daze. I swallowed hard and closed my eyes, but I had nothing to fear for the shield disabler let us slip right through without a hiccup. There were no breaks in the generator, which outlined the circumference of the force field like a speed bump, so Cass had to ease the truck over the large black bump. I thought the truck would crack it, but it didn't even bend. I looked at it out the back window and saw tiny, blinking green lights running along the bottom.

We turned into a shadowy alleyway and stopped to get our bearings, before continuing on. I was finally back in the city I had abandoned as a child. The evening sunlight penetrated the shield, casting a beautiful medley of different colours over the imprisoned city. My jaw dropped at the awe-inspiring sight. The city was filled with people going about their evening routines. It had been so long since I'd been one of them, but as I studied the faces of the people walking around, I could sense the heaviness of oppression etched in their stone-like features.

"No, these people are safe because of you. They're grateful for you. You control their whole lives, their whole world, and they're much better for it."

Alex handed me a large gray hoodie and jogging pants from his backpack. "They can't see our robotic parts, and you'll have to try to keep your face hidden. And tie back your hair. It's a dead giveaway." He reached into his bag and handed sunglasses to Tolli and Cass. He put on an old baseball cap and shoved another one at Tolli. He reached into the bag once again and hesitated slightly before pulling out a straw fedora complete with a blue ribbon and looked at Cass.

She glared at it with disgust. "Seriously?!"

Alex shrugged apologetically, "I thought it was nice."

"It's not."

Tolli and I tried to hold our laughter in, to no avail.

I slipped on the clothes over my shorts and tank top, carefully covering every inch of gleaming metal, and Alex did the same with his extra clothes. It was hot in the truck, so I was grateful we'd put on our disguises at the last possible moment. I could already feel my body heating up and sweat collecting on my forehead. With my hands in my pockets and my face cast downward, shrouded under the hood of my sweatshirt, I was unrecognizable. I would appear to be a shy teenager in clothes a couple sizes too big. A nobody.

"Wait, where are we going to park this thing?" Cass questioned.

Alex's hazel eyes locked onto the back of Tolli's head, who scratched his chin before answering, "Don't worry. I think I know a guy."

I stared at the street ahead of us. I tried to remember the stores I had visited as a child. Cars whizzed by us in flashes of black, blue, and silver. I thought back to the last time I'd driven down a street.

That was when...when we had gotten into the car accident.

Suddenly, the sound of zooming vehicles and screeching tires made my body freeze, and my throat constricted, cutting off my air supply. That was the day everything had changed for me.

Somebody grabbed my hand, and my first instinct was to shake them off, but when I looked down and realized who it was, I stopped myself. I felt embarrassed by the show of weakness. Cass had reached back and squeezed my hand. She moved her hand back to the steering wheel and smiled at me in the rear-view mirror.

Tolli gave Cass directions to a decrepit old shop with blinds draped over the front windows. He directed her around to the back where a few rusty garage doors were spread out along the back wall of the building. We stopped and waited for a few seconds in front of one of the doors and looked around. The door eased open and out walked a rough-looking man. His features were similar to Tolli's with his mess of golden hair and light blue eyes.

He sauntered up to our truck and his suspicious gaze fell on Tolli. Disbelief showed in his eyes. "Trevy?" Then his eyes crinkled, his expression softened, and his mouth spread into a big smile. Using the back of his hand, he wiped the sweat off his forehead, leaving a trail of grease behind. His overalls were torn, and he hadn't bothered to do the straps up, so they hung by his sides. His brown tank top was on backwards, with the tag sticking out at his collarbone.

We cautiously piled out of the truck.

Tolli sighed, "Guys, this is my brother, Aar—"

"Ace," the man corrected. "Welcome to Ace's Garage."

Ace grinned widely and playfully put Tolli in a headlock before letting him loose and slapping him hard on the back repeatedly. The rest of us watched in amusement. Ace was a taller, skinnier version of Tolli. I noticed a large tattoo of a snake on his shoulder: an inky serpent coiled around an ace of spades.

"Did you steal this truck, Trevy?" Ace asked, curiously examining the rusty truck and running his finger along the side door. "We're a legit garage now. Not a lot of room to commit crimes around here anymore." He awkwardly waited for Tolli's reaction, inclining his head and widening his big blue eyes. "I feel like we've switched roles."

Tolli ignored his antics and straightened his shoulders. "I did what I had to," he mumbled, staring blankly into the distance before turning to his brother. "Aaron, we need to park our truck here for a little while. We'll come back for it soon."

Ace nodded slightly. He looked like he had a million questions for Tolli, but he didn't say anything more. Instead, Ace looked around at the rest of us. "Who's the foxy babe?" he asked, cocking his eyebrow at Cass. "Hard to believe you'd be hanging around with the likes of Trevy," he said with a wink and a grin.

She pulled off her sunglasses and glared at him while Alex and I backed into the shadows of the garage, hoping Ace wouldn't pay any attention to us. I tugged my hood forward and looked down as Alex positioned himself slightly in front of me.

Ace strolled over to Cass. "What's a pretty little lady like you doing with my ugly brother?"

She stepped closer to him and narrowed her eyes. The top of her head barely reached the tattooed snake on Ace's shoulder.

Tolli's eyes grew wide as he sensed what was about to happen and tried to intervene, "Vee, settle down. Aaron, watch your mouth, she's..."

Cass cut him off by throwing a sucker punch directly into Ace's stomach, and he staggered back. He stayed hunched over to catch his breath. I suppressed a giggle underneath my hood and exchanged a quick smile with Alex. Ace didn't stand a chance.

"A fighter," Tolli sighed.

Ace groaned, "Man, she punches way harder than you."

Cass flicked the dark hair peeking out beneath her fedora and announced, "We'll be leaving now." She swivelled on her heels and walked out while Ace shook his head and watched her with a smile, impressed.

The rest of us darted to catch up to her.

May 27, 2070, 5:00 pm...

Wren's security headquarters weren't too difficult to find. Just an hour's walk away from Ace's garage, her towering fortress loomed over all the other buildings around it, and its shadow stretched across everything that dared cross its path. Numerous full-sized glass panels lined the walls on each floor. Balconies on the higher floors overlooked the whole city. The roof was peaked on one side and resembled a right triangle. It was very "Wren" in its unique design.

We stopped about half a block away and sat down on a bench, trying to give the impression we were a group of friends hanging out. We positioned ourselves so Alex could have a clear view of the front of the building.

"The front entrance is heavily guarded," he murmured.

"Great, that's my favourite formation," Tolli quipped.

Alex continued, "They must be in the midst of a shift change. There are quite a few security guards leaving the building now."

Cass turned slightly and squinted her eyes, watching a young security guard walk out the doors. Even from a distance, he looked jittery and nervous. His posture was a little crooked, which mimicked his nose, and he had black beady eyes. Freckles dotted his cheeks and made him look like a kid. A small blue and gray backpack hung from his shoulder.

Cass swivelled around to whisper to us, "Meet me back here in exactly one hour. You guys look for a way in." Then her mood shifted as she turned around, grinning and running to catch up to the security guard.

As she ran, she yelled out, "Hey, Earl! Wow, I haven't seen you in so long!"

He jumped and looked at her. "Uh…my name's not Earl."

Cass didn't hesitate for a second as she jogged over to him and gave him a friendly pat on the back. He looked uncomfortable, but Cass never stopped chatting, and the two of them eventually walked down the street together. Cass's friendly voice grew fainter and fainter.

"What does she see in him?" Tolli asked sarcastically.

Alex put his arm around Tolli and pulled him toward the building. "Don't worry, Tolli. She'll be back. I can't see it working out with Earl." He chuckled. "Now, let's take a quick stroll in front of the building and look for a way in."

I followed them as the side of the building came into view, but there were no easy entry points, and groups of guards were visible through the windows.

"No good. And the back is completely fenced in. Let's keep walking and check out the other side."

After scrutinizing the front of the building, Alex ushered us into a bakery across the street, and we sat down by the window. Our hasty disguises should keep future Wren from recognizing us with any of her security cameras, but I was still alert and on edge. What if my future self already knew we were here?

As I scanned the building from my new vantage point, I spotted something that reflected the sun into my eyes. I shielded my eyes with my hand and strained to focus in on this side of the building.

"There's a metal thingy up there that leads to stairs." Tolli said what was on my mind.

"That's very helpful," Alex teased, then added as an after thought, "Hey, we could use that. It's a fire escape."

"That's it. That's our way in," I whispered excitedly.

"Are you sure you want to do this? It's not too late to turn back."

I shook my head in an effort to shut the voice up.

"We'll still need to get through the glass though. I'm willing to bet it won't be single pane." Alex thought out loud.

Tolli stared out the window and bit his bottom lip. "I'll meet you guys in a bit." Before we could say another word, he jumped up and ran out the door, his golden mane flying.

"We'll get in, no problem." Alex smiled reassuringly at me. "Now, let's get out of here. We'll come back when it's time to meet them."

"Nice watch." I pointed at the white strap on Alex's wrist, looking for something to distract us. We had some time to kill, so we'd sat down on the bench again. I wasn't completely sure what Cass and Tolli were up to, but I had my suspicions.

Alex had taken off his backpack and his sleeve had slipped up, revealing the white watch strap.

He took the bait and smiled. "This watch was a gift from your uncle. Rob had been teaching me how to tell time when I first stayed with them, so William had surprised me with this."

The clock's face was outlined with silver, and the strap was now more of an off-white with age. Alex took it off and showed me the engraving on the back.

He read the inscription out loud: "To Alex ~ *Aut viam inveniam aut faciam.* ~ W.D. It's Latin for 'I will either find a way or make one.'"

"Exactly. *Even your uncle knew. I will always find a way.*"

I smiled with sad appreciation and added, "That sounds like him. He loved Latin phrases. It's beautiful." I handed it back.

"What if it doesn't work?" I finally asked the question bouncing around in my head.

Alex leaned back and put his watch back on. "*Aut viam inveniam aut faciam.*"

"And if that isn't enough?"

"It will be. It has to be."

I squeezed my eyes shut and imagined all the possible outcomes. Everything had to go perfectly, and I hoped we weren't wasting our time.

"Hey, Donahue! You were right! She did come back." Tolli shouted as he sauntered toward us over an hour later.

Cass looked at Tolli in confusion as she, too, made her way toward us. "What are you two talking about?"

"Nothing," Tolli said as he smiled and shifted the small messenger bag on his shoulder. He was still breathing heavily from his run, and sweat was soaking through his t-shirt.

"You guys are late," Alex accused, but he sounded relieved.

"Sorry," Cass apologized, "But I got some kind of security pass."

"Awesome." Tolli gave her two thumbs up. "No doubt we'll need it after I use this." He patted his bag.

Alex surveyed the building across the street, and then he added, "But we'll need to wait until it gets darker to make our move."

I followed his gaze and noticed a camera directed at the front of the building.

"I saw a diner down the street," Cass suggested. "C'mon, dinner's on me!"

She just shrugged when we all looked at her suspiciously.

"Uh, Vee, what did you do to Earl?" Tolli asked.

She smirked. "Don't worry about Earl. He's been working very hard lately and needed a little nap."

We were too hungry to ask any more questions.

3 HOURS and 49 MINUTES to SILEO TERRA

May 27, 2070, 8:11 pm...

It was time. The sun had set now, and the wisps of gold that had lingered in the sky had finally disappeared, giving way to the darkness we were waiting for. Dark clouds formed above us, but fortunately, the faint magenta glow from the bubble shield lit our way, and we made our way back to Wren's headquarters without being recognized or stopped. If we slipped in fast, we would have more time before the guards found us.

Alex placed his metallic hand on the wall and took a deep breath. He gathered his strength, took a few long steps backward, and then sprinted toward the wall. He leapt up onto the side of the building and pushed himself back and forth, using the wall of the next building to get higher and higher. I was impressed by his abilities.

He was dangling from the ladder when Tolli softly called up, "Ya good?"

Alex swung up onto the deck and lowered the ladder as far as it would go. Tolli reached up and grabbed it, and Cass used his shoulders to climb up onto the ladder. He handed me the heavy messenger bag and helped me up next.

I cautiously followed Cass up while Alex slid down past me to help pull Tolli up.

"Are you sure you're choosing the right side?"

We were vigilant as we ascended the ladder, careful not to make any noise. Cass stopped next to a window on the fourth floor and pointed to it.

Tolli pulled out a pair of gloves, safety goggles, a pair of large suction cups, and a glass cutter from the bag.

"Whoa, where did you get all that stuff?" Cass looked impressed as she cocked an eyebrow.

Tolli looked over at Cass with a serious expression on his face. "Do you really want to know?" he asked tersely and stared at her for a few seconds before falling back into his usual jolly disposition and scoffed, "It's actually yours. Ace sends his love." With a silly grin on his face, he started efficiently cutting away at the glass.

The combination of our stress level and the look on Cass's face made Alex and I stifle a burst of laughter as we clamped our hands over our mouths in a desperate attempt to stay quiet.

As Alex and I regained our composure, Tolli removed a circular piece of glass, making sure it didn't fall, and we scrambled into the building in single file.

"You don't want to do this."

Cass smiled and shook her head. "You three are unbelievable."

We were inside. After blindly making our way through a darkened, empty room, we crept down the dark corridor, trying to stay in the blind spots of the cameras. I could faintly see the outlines of the others and the blinking lights of the cameras sweeping back and forth.

I tensed when Cass patted me on the shoulder and gave my arm a squeeze. "There's a side exit on the ground floor directly below us. Meet us there as soon as you can, and good luck. We have to keep our distance since she'll most likely kill us on sight."

I gave her a big, fake grin to hide my nervousness.

Tolli added, "There will be cameras in every room…" He looked around and immediately pointed at a large workspace visible through the window of a door up ahead. "Try that room. It looks bigger, and you might need some room to move. If Wren is here, she'll eventually hear of a lookalike in the building. Maybe she already has. We'll try to draw the guards away, so you have a better chance of Wren approaching you alone. Either way, I'm sure she'll want to see you face to face in the end."

"You can't fight me. You don't stand a chance." I squeezed my eyes shut tightly and took a deep breath, doing my best to ignore the voice in my head.

We followed him to the door, and Cass smiled as she pulled the security pass out of her back pocket and pressed it into the panel beside the door. The card was oddly shaped. Instead of a rectangle, it had five sides. I guessed the card must only be able to open select doors in the building because the key panels on the other doors were shaped differently.

Cass walked into the room, and the lights turned on automatically, revealing a bunch of cubicles. The desks were cluttered with papers, file folders, and high-tech equipment.

As I looked around, I pressed my hands against my temples and screamed silently in my head. The anxious feeling that had begun hours earlier was now painfully gnawing at my stomach. A shiver crawled up my spine when I spotted familiar dents on the back wall.

Alex placed his hand on my back to get my attention. He whispered in my ear, "We believe in you. See you soon." The three of them ran out, leaving me all alone.

"I won't leave you."

2 HOURS and 55 MINUTES to SILEO TERRA

May 27, 2070, 9:05 pm...

There were only two outcomes to this story. I would either die or emerge victorious. Only one of us could win. I clenched my fist around the orb.

"You really think you can—"

"Who are you?"

I jumped and spun around. I hadn't heard anyone come in. She must have teleported into the room. Horror and dread filled me when I saw my reflection in the face of the person standing in front of me. I was looking straight into my own eyes. Her familiar red locks fell over her face, and my robotic parts also crawled across her skin. She looked like me, but as I stared into her eyes, I found nothing recognizable in them.

I forgot every line I had rehearsed in my head. "You need to stop." My voice was weak and pathetic, and my entire body was trembling.

"Why do you look like me?" she muttered under her breath.

"You can't make everyone live in your cage."

"A shield is not a cage."

She repeated her question, "Who are you?" It suddenly dawned on me that her eyes were not the same as mine. Her irises glowed the same brilliant blue as the orb, and her gaze was piercing.

The energy in the air was palpable, and it made my head spin. Black dots danced in my vision. Through the yelling and the chaos in my head, I heard my own strained voice, "I'm you. Past you. I came here to tell you that you've made a terrible mistake."

"Mistake?" she laughed. "I don't make mistakes." Suddenly, she disappeared. I heard her voice behind me. "*We* don't make mistakes." She slowly paced around me, looking me up and down. "I can hear your heart racing. Why is it beating so fast? Are you frightened?"

I didn't reply. She smiled mockingly, then both her and the voice in my head spoke in unison, "*It beats in tune with mine. We are one and the same.*"

A lump rose in my throat. I tried to move away from her, but my limbs were heavy and frozen with fear. Even my mind felt frozen as I struggled against the pull of the orb to try and string words together to make a sentence. "No, we aren't. That thing, that orb, has pushed you over the edge. You're insane; you need help."

She started nodding her head. "The time machine," she mumbled. "Someone got it to work. Was it that boy?"

I started to panic when she mentioned Alex. "Look, I know you, and I know you want to control your life. I know you want to eliminate any possibility of anything or anyone hurting you ever again. I know you want safety and security, but you're slowly destroying everyone's freedom along the way. You've done whatever you had to do to work your way to the top, to make your vision of security a reality. But life was never intended to work that way! Why won't you stop and listen?"

"*We will never stop.*" I wasn't sure whose voice it was this time.

"I'll tell you this just one more time: YOU NEED TO STOP!" I shouted in sudden rage and desperation.

"Or what? Are you going to make me?" She chuckled, pushing her hair away from her face so she could look me in the eyes. "I am safety. I am power. I am control. My powers make me who I am. I will never stop. I will never give it up."

"I need it. It's mine...my uncle's. I will never give it up." The familiar words echoed eerily in my head. I had said those words about the orb in my pocket too.

Dread flooded my heart as I finally recognized myself in her: the fear, the confusion, the obsession. She was trying to be the hero of her own story. I noticed she looked utterly exhausted, as though time itself had continually added to the burden she had to carry. Her face was ghostly pale, making the dark rings around her eyes even more visible. Like me, she had endured the death of her parents and her uncle right before her eyes. Both of us had been affected by the orb, but only she had experienced the full consequences of succumbing to its power.

"Now ask yourself: which of you is better?"

"Shut up!" I wasn't sure who I was yelling at.

I reached down into the deepest part of me and forced myself to continue. "No, you hurt the friends who treated you like family. Aren't you tired of all this?" I pleaded, gesturing all around us. "Your attempt to control and protect will never end. Every time you achieve control in one area, you lose it in another. You are trying to control the uncontrollable. I see that. I understand that now. Aren't you exhausted?"

She gave no response, but she closed her eyes and pinched her bottom lip with her thumb and index finger.

"You can't keep everyone safe by locking them up. I understand what you're trying to do, and it won't work. You're trying to keep yourself and others from feeling more pain and loss. I know you weren't responsible for what happened to Mom and Dad or Uncle William. You couldn't have stopped it. And you can't stop bad things from happening in the world," I whispered.

"Enough! We're done talking. You have to go now."

"Goodbye, Wren."

Cold sweat trickled down my forehead. I was pretty sure she didn't mean I had to turn around and leave the building. This was not going well, and I weakly replied, "You can't kill me."

She smirked and replied, "Who said I was going to kill you?" And after a haunting cackle, she continued, "There are other ways of controlling your destiny!" She vanished and then reappeared behind me. She repeated herself, "You have to go now." I swivelled around to face her and saw blue bolts of electricity crackle around her fingertips, seeping into the creases of metal on her hands. She was bathed in her superhuman power, and she looked unstoppable.

I grew dizzy as the voice added, *"You could've had it ALL."*

She inched toward me and I instinctively backed up, tripping on a cardboard box and crashing to the floor. I was stunned momentarily, and the only thing that moved was my chest, trying to catch my breath. It was time for Plan B. I raised my arms defensively, then lowered and opened one hand to reveal the orb's radiant glow. I struggled to sit up while holding it out to her in my palm.

She froze, shocked, and then gasped, "My orb." It mesmerized her, drawing her in with each passing second. The lightening around her subsided, and she walked closer. My future self had already merged with the orb, so she had forgotten what it was like to hold its power in her hand. She reached out; her hand hovered inches above mine. I didn't move, resisting the urge to close my fist.

My voice was hoarse, "This was the only thing that survived the car crash. It was Uncle William's. Now it's ours."

"You've made the right decision."

Her voice was now also a soft whisper, "Give it to me. I need it."

"I'll give it to you," I promised.

"Yes, yes, yesssss." The orb pulsed in my palm.

I grabbed her outstretched hand in mine, the orb sandwiched between our palms. I held on firmly with both hands, refusing to let go even as she tried to pull back. Only one of us could win. Only one of us would survive.

"What have you done?!"

I whispered, "Two identical objects cannot occupy the same space at the same time." That was what Alex had summarized it down to after trying to explain quantum physics to me and then laughing at the blank look in my eyes. It was the Plan B we hadn't told the others about, the plan that didn't have a concrete ending, the plan where I had to give up control and take the chance that I could be the one who wouldn't survive.

Screams filled the room, making my head pound. I couldn't tell if it was coming from me, future Wren, the orb, or all three of us.

The orb sparked like it was being electrocuted. It was deciding which one of us would be banned from existence.

After a few seconds, her hand began to distort and mix with the glowing light of the orb. The blue from her eyes dimmed, and I saw familiar green eyes staring at me. She looked scared.

"You are the better one."

"There was no other way. Your time is almost up," I sadly told her as she started to fade. Her eyes were wide with fear, and her body was frozen from the contact with the orb's power. I continued, "You chose this."

She grew pale, then translucent, but made no sound. Finally, she closed her eyes and whispered with her last breath, "You chose this too." I was left staring at the orb in my metal palm as she disappeared completely.

The sound of a ticking clock on the wall tore my attention away from the orb and reminded me my time was almost up too.

2 HOURS and 38 MINUTES to SILEO TERRA

May 27, 2070, 9:22 pm...

As I pocketed the orb, I felt the floor tremble and realized I had to move fast, so I sprinted back to my friends. I felt as though my limbs were made of concrete, like it had taken days to defeat myself instead of just minutes. I couldn't seem to run fast enough. My shoes crushed pieces of the ceiling that had already begun to fall in my path, and my footsteps were drowned out by the groaning of the structure falling apart all around me. The timeline was collapsing on itself, slowly destroying everything. Jagged shards of glass around the broken windows gleamed in the fading fluorescent light that flickered on and off. Only a few windows had been left undamaged on this side of the building. I fled down the wide hallway and down the stairs.

As I approached the main floor, the walls began to crumble around me. The small pieces of drywall and sawdust from the ceiling that had been falling began to give way to large chunks of wood and concrete. I ran on, coughing from the cloud of dust growing bigger by the second. A beam crashed down in front of me, and I leapt over it just in time. Even with all the noise of the collapsing building around me, I heard shouts and banging behind the door that led to the rendezvous point near our planned exit.

I got to the door and pushed hard against it, but it wouldn't budge. Bracing myself, I ripped the metal door from its hinges and raised it slightly in the air to throw it aside. I called out, "Guys? I did it!" As soon as I said those words, a flash of blue swam across my eyes and the seams along my robotic hands. I blinked quickly.

A group of security guards in black uniforms turned around to look at me and we all froze. All their weapons were drawn and pointed at Alex, Tolli, and Cass. Tolli had a swollen eye, and rather than paying attention to me, two other guards were still kicking and punching Alex, trying to subdue him.

Then those guards stopped too when they realized things had gone quiet, and confusion washed over their faces. For a second, no one moved. The floor began rumbling and groaning again, snapping us out of our trance. Then everything turned into chaos. Cass sprang up to forcefully relieve the guards nearest her of their weapons as Alex freed himself and kicked a guard in the stomach, sending him flying backward. Tolli elbowed a guard in the jaw so hard I swore I heard bone breaking. I still had the door in my hands, so I hurried over to help shield my friends from incoming bullets.

After the guards fired a few shots at us, they hesitated. I peeked out from behind the door I was holding, challenging their piercing gazes. A woman with dark skin and thin, long braids pointed an accusing finger at me. "She's an imposter! Look, her eyes aren't glowing blue!"

"She's with them!" hollered a male guard.

"What happened to the real Wren Derecho?" another guard chimed in.

I hurled the metal door as hard as I could, sending it crashing into several black figures. A stocky guard lunged at me, but I nimbly ducked to one side and slipped out of his grasp. I backhanded him across the side of his head and knew by the sound it made I wouldn't have to worry about him anymore. I turned and punched the guard who'd called me an imposter in the stomach.

Alex grabbed his backpack from the ground and drew a pistol-like weapon from it, which made the remaining guards freeze. I hadn't seen it since he'd used it to destroy my safe, and its navy-blue, narrow barrel reminded me of a time that now seemed like a dream. Alex pulled the trigger repeatedly, aiming just above the group of guards, and yelled for us to start running. The four of us took off sprinting as the guards took cover.

"What was that all about?" I shouted as we approached our exit and dodged a light crashing down overhead, causing sparks to fly in every direction.

"We were creating a distraction," Cass responded nonchalantly and then shot a worried glance at Tolli. She had lost her fedora in the fight, so her hair flew around her face as she ran. Tolli's right eye was now so swollen he could barely see out of it. I knew their plan of distraction had come with a cost.

We finally made it out of the building. "We don't have much time," Alex's eyes darted up at the collapsing structure. Blood dripped from a cut on his forehead as he took off his watch and placed it in my hand. He looked at me proudly. "I knew you could do it, Wren. Now, we need to get you back to Tempus!"

The voices of the guards grew fainter as we sprinted away, but the bullets still rang out and ricocheted close to us. We raced down the streets, dodging falling debris and working hard to keep our balance as the world all around us began to crumble.

We turned a corner just as a lamppost smashed down behind us. Tolli rushed forward to take the lead. "Ace's garage is that way!" he ordered as we sprinted across the empty street. The wind picked up, blowing sand and dust that stung my eyes. We darted past a half-collapsed library and kept running until we began to recognize buildings we'd passed earlier. We arrived at the street corner where Ace's garage still stood, barely holding together, and rounded the corner to the back; however, Ace was nowhere to be found.

Tolli stopped abruptly in front of his brother's opened garage.

"No!" he yelled in frustration.

Ace's garage was completely bare; not even a ghost lingered within the walls.

The ground began to shake beneath us, and at first, I thought it was another tremor. "The shield's coming down!" I yelled at the others when I realized what it really was. The pinky purple glow of the shield above us glitched like static on a TV and spat out electrical sparks like rain. They felt like small pinpricks when they landed on my skin, but I paid no attention to them.

"Quick!" Tolli yelled at us, then added, "We need to find a vehicle!" He ran back to the front of the garage and glanced up and down the street.

A parked blue convertible crumbled to the ground right before our eyes and behind it, the growing figures of the security guards were coming closer and closer. We raced down the street to avoid being shot. The zinging bullets were barely audible over the overwhelming noise of shattering glass, crumbling brick, and buzzing from the shield as it began losing power. I felt a bullet ricochet off my metallic hand, not even making a mark on the fortified metal.

Tolli led the way, making random turns to try and lose the guards. When he felt we had enough time, he turned down an alley and stopped at the first car he saw. Tolli picked up one of many rocks that littered the ground and chucked it at the window, completely shattering the glass.

Alex tossed his weapon to Cass and pulled an identical one from his backpack. I watched as the beam from Cass's weapon zapped a guard in the shoulder. They were buying time for Tolli to get the SUV started.

Tolli was lying on the driver's seat, now littered with shattered glass from the window he had broken. I winced at the thought of the glass cutting into his back.

"Wren, I need a screwdriver!"

I looked over at Alex and pulled the backpack off his shoulders. He lost his balance momentarily but managed to catch himself while still aiming and firing at the guards. I dumped the entire contents onto the concrete. There weren't many things left in it, and there definitely wasn't a screwdriver. It must have fallen out. I stood back up and pulled Tolli from the seat and demanded, "Where are the screws?"

He pointed out three screws under the steering wheel. I dug my fingers into both sides of the plastic cover, the seams of my metallic hands once again burning a bright blue. I ripped the entire thing off, including the screws. Tolli raised his eyebrows then simply waved his hand for me to move out of the way. With the plastic cover removed, a mess of wires splayed out, and it seemed impossible to work with, but Tolli obviously knew what he was doing. He grabbed a small knife from his pocket and went to work.

With my heart threatening to burst out of my chest, I bent over and stuffed everything back in the bag, still ducking the gunfire and watching the cracking of the concrete beneath my feet.

"Anytime now, Tolli!" Cass called out.

At the same time, Alex exclaimed, "I'm out!" and turned around to climb into the car. I threw his backpack into the back seat while he jumped into the front passenger seat.

Frustrated, Tolli muttered through clenched teeth, "Come on! Start!"

Immediately, the engine roared to life, and I leapt into the back seat. Cass retreated from her post and waited to jump into the driver's seat.

Tolli leapt out of the car, gripped the car door I had just opened, and was about to follow me in. I noticed his hands were burned and calloused, and I looked up to see his pale eyes staring blankly at me. His shaggy blonde locks fell over his face, and he stumbled forward, causing the door to slam shut. I gasped as he looked down and put a hand to his chest. Dark blood seeped through the front of his shirt.

"Go," he whispered to Cass through gritted teeth as she looked out her broken window. Blood smeared on my window as he leaned against it. "GO!" He yelled before falling to the ground.

Cass and Alex exchanged grim looks and nodded slightly.

"We can't leave him!" I screamed and went to open the door, but Cass pushed a button and the lock clicked.

I put my hands against the window and looked down, sobbing and shaking my head. Tolli's eyes were still open, and he looked directly at me, his chest painfully rising and falling to the beat of the pulse in my throat. A dark red pool grew around him. He smiled and mouthed, "It's okay," before his eyelids fluttered closed and we sped off.

I reefed on the handle and it broke off in my hand. I leaned my head against the window and screamed, "NO!"

"We didn't have a choice. This is all about you, Wren," Cass said gently but firmly. From the wobble in her voice, I knew she was saying it to all of us.

We zoomed down the street as the pavement began to crack all around us. We hit a bump in the asphalt and lurched forward, causing my head to smash against the roof. I didn't even feel the pain.

I looked back to see the security guards' silhouettes gathering around Tolli's body. It was dark, but the streetlights allowed me to see one of the security guards aiming his pistol at Tolli's head. The flash of the gunshot made me cringe. I buried my head in my arms and sobbed uncontrollably.

Now, there were only three of us left.

40 MINUTES to SILEO TERRA

May 27, 2070, 11:20 pm...

"Time will eventually take us all." My uncle had said that once.

The truth he spoke rang in my head, and Cass's words echoed in my thoughts, "This is all about you, Wren."

All of this was about me. This world I had created had been paid for with blood and destruction and years of captivity. And now, it could take us all down with it.

The shield was slowly malfunctioning, which gave us a better chance of escaping without our shield disabler. Unfortunately, we still had to get to it before it came crashing down on us.

"We just need to get to the edge of the city." Cass sounded cool and composed, as though we hadn't just left Tolli to die in a pool of his own blood surrounded by hostile guards. Alex, however, remained silent.

We turned a sharp corner, and I felt the vehicle lift on its two left wheels. I could see Ashborne's city limits coming up. The shield's generator was glitching even more now, flickering on and off, and electric sparks exploded all along it. The generator surrounded the whole city, but it wasn't even a foot tall. It still looked like a huge speed bump, now haphazardly shooting out deadly pink rays that would fry anything or anyone.

Cass glanced up at the rear-view mirror and exclaimed in a panicked voice, "You've got to be kidding me!"

I turned around to look out the back window and saw a black truck with flashing lights racing after us.

Cass made another sharp turn, screeching the worn tires of the car. "Why did you turn?" I shouted in frustration.

"We need to lose them! The shield isn't quite down yet; we can't get through!" Cass's usually calm voice was now filled with frustration, fear, and grief.

She circled several blocks until we were back at the same point again, but the shield was still not fully disabled. I could see sections no longer functioning, allowing the darkness to seep through, but we still couldn't get through it. Cass spun the wheel and stepped on the gas, and we circled around once again. The black truck had turned off its flashing lights, but I could still see its headlights occasionally through the back window. More trucks joined the chase. Now we had a good-sized team hunting us down.

Suddenly, the rumbling in the ground intensified, creating a large crack in the generator. Cass took the opportunity and stomped on the gas pedal. I held my breath and braced myself for the impact as we hit the shield generator hard. The backpack beside me toppled over, spilling its contents on the floor beside me. We were out. I slowly exhaled.

"Everyone okay?" Alex finally spoke in the darkness, and Cass flipped on the headlights. It illuminated the outline of their heads, and their eyes seemed eerie and black when they turned to look back at me.

"Yeah, I'm good," I muttered.

CRASH! A bullet smashed through the back window and exited through the front windshield, nearly hitting Alex. I ducked down against my seat and stayed there. My heart pounded in my throat as I realized the black trucks had followed us out of the city.

"Cut the lights!" I yelled.

"What?!" Cass exclaimed.

Alex agreed with me, "Turn the lights off, and then stop somewhere to let them go by. We can't let them follow us to the warehouse."

Another bullet slammed into the back windshield, causing the whole thing to shatter. Automatically, I threw my hands around my head to avoid getting cut by the falling glass. I crouched forward and gripped the back of Alex's seat, still trying to keep my head down.

"Do it, Vee," Alex encouraged gently, "You're the best driver I know. You could get back to the warehouse blindfolded. Do it quickly. We're almost there."

Vee shut off the lights, plunging us into the darkness of the night. Only the headlights of the black trucks were visible now. Cass sped up and then veered off the main road, driving for a while before sliding into a slot between a few leafy trees in one smooth movement. The black trucks whizzed by a minute later.

I counted to sixty and then whispered, "I think we're all clear."

There was no answer and the vehicle lurched forward.

"Vee?" I heard Alex's concerned voice. "I think you might be able to turn the lights back on."

The car's engine roared and we zoomed forward on the bumpy terrain in the dark.

"Cass?!" I yelled, panicking. Something was wrong.

Alex flipped on the interior light. Cass was unconscious, her head lolling on her chest and her foot still pressed down on the gas pedal. Alex awkwardly shoved her foot off the pedal and managed to slam his foot on the brake. We jolted to a sudden stop, and Alex put the SUV into park.

Alex jumped out of the SUV and flung open the drivers' side door. He carefully lifted Cass out as I used my metallic hand to sweep as much glass off the back seat as I could. Alex opened the back door and laid Cass down next to me. He took her place in the driver's seat and put the vehicle in reverse.

"Try to wake her up," Alex ordered as he glanced back at us for a moment.

I propped Cass's head on my lap and placed my finger on her throat to check her pulse.

"Alex, I don't think she's breathing!" I shouted in a panic, shock and dread overtaking my body. Just then, Cass shifted her head slightly with a gasp, her breathing light and sporadic. I brushed her hair away from her face and breathed a sigh of relief before announcing, "She's awake!"

Cass looked up and wrapped her arms around me loosely. "I…feel funny."

I cradled her like a baby. "It'll be okay," I lied and hugged her close.

She inhaled heavily, then exhaled, and I felt her weight on me lessen.

"Hurry," she whispered her final word to us before she breathed her last breath. She faded into thin air, disintegrating along with the rest of the world. I clenched my empty hands into fists and felt hot tears roll down my cheeks.

I choked out, "Alex, she's gone." And then I wept.

Now, there were only two of us left.

11 MINUTES
to SILEO TERRA

May 27, 2070, 11:49 pm...

Alex and I burst through the door to the main workroom where Tempus III stood resolute. There was no time to lose. We'd already wasted time losing the guards. Alex flung open the metal door and I followed him in. He tapped on the screen at the control desk, sweat dripping down the side of his face. Words and images popped up and closed faster than my brain could register them, and his fingers were a blur of motion as he programmed the machine.

I sat down to catch my breath, clutching the watch Alex had given me, and noticed its glass face had cracked.

"I will stay with you," the voice in my head whispered, *"Alex can never promise you that."*

"Alex, come with me," I pleaded as I looked over at him. I thought of all the pain he had endured. It wasn't too late to change it. He understood me. I didn't want to lose him.

"He won't stay with you."

Alex hesitated before entering the final commands. He sighed, "Wren, we both know I can't."

"But, Alex, you'll..." I pressed my trembling lips together, heartbroken thinking of his fate. "You'll die like Tolli, like Cass."

"You can depend on me."

Alex lifted his fingers away from the control desk and ran them through his dark curls, trying to find the right words. Finally, he managed in a thick voice, "I'm where I'm supposed to be, Wren."

I looked at him with tear-filled eyes but stayed silent.

"And you're where you're supposed to be."

Alex turned to leave but I cried out, "Wait!" and stood up.

He stopped and looked at me sadly. A single tear dripped down my cheek as I held my hand out to him.

My voice shook but I managed to whisper, "T-take it."

"What are you doing? I am your source of control! I give you all your power! YOU NEED ME!"

I bit my lip and I pushed him out the door, closing it before either of us could react to what I had just done. I watched through the window as Alex stared down at the orb that now sat in his robotic fingers. I felt a piece of me had been ripped away, leaving me to die a slow death. His outstretched hand trembled.

The voice in my head screamed at me, *"You'll regret this moment for eternity!"*

I shook my head. I murmured, "No. I will regret many things, but this will not be one of them."

"You are nothing without me!"

"Maybe, but maybe you're nothing without me."

I squeezed the watch in my fist, replacing the familiar object I had held so dear to my heart. The orb was gone for good, and it felt like a huge burden had been lifted off my shoulders. I waited, but the voice had now ceased to exist.

Alex finally looked up at me and smiled. He waved goodbye and shouted loud enough for me to hear through the glass, "Look for me!"

The time on the watch read midnight, and then everything outside started fading into nothing.

≋ SILEO TERRA ACTIVATED

Unknown date, unknown time...

I watched as the warehouse disintegrated outside the time machine's window, sucking everything in, including the old SUV we had stolen, in a whirlwind of destruction. The roof of the warehouse crumbled away so I could see the world around me. From skyscrapers to small shops, time was destroying everything. I strained to catch a last glimpse of Alex; his hazel eyes never looked away from me as the time machine lifted farther from the ground. He continued to comfort me with his warm smile until he and the orb in his palm faded away.

Only I was left.

The future I had just been standing in was now gone. I hurtled through the threads of time and could not help but notice the broken shards of the collapsed timeline swirling everywhere, threatening to knock Tempus III off course.

"Will the past even exist anymore?" I thought out loud as seconds seemed to turn into hours, and I waited uncertainly to return to my present.

I was free of the orb's control, and with my freedom, my future was being rewritten. It came at a great cost, losing three people I deeply cared about. They wouldn't know me when I returned, and in a way, I wouldn't know them either. Now a new future awaited me, and I had no idea what to expect. I didn't even know what I wanted anymore, now that my obsession with the orb and my desperate need to time travel were gone.

I sat down at the control desk, but I didn't need to do anything as Tempus III knew where I needed to go. I needed to go home.

The creaks and groans of the machine were a warning that it, too, would disintegrate soon since it was also from a future that no longer existed. I gazed out the window as the threads of time whizzed by and a broken shard of time scraped its jagged edge along the side of Tempus III, peeling the metal away from the sides of the machine. The threads of time had never looked so beautiful, with their painted flashes of deep purples and bright pinks marking the finish line of the race between me and time itself.

When I finally caught my breath, it dawned on me that I had won. I was overwhelmed with sorrow, joy, and relief. I was finally going home. I leaned back against my chair and closed my eyes.

⇛ SILEO TERRA COMPLETE

October 1, 2059, 3:43 pm...

An eternity had passed and yet, nothing had happened. Tempus III began to fade around me. The floor gave way, and I was falling. Falling. Falling. In the darkness, I squeezed my eyes shut as the wind tore at my hair and clothes. Finally, I landed roughly on something hard and cold.

I opened my eyes and hesitantly looked around my room. I was back in the present after coming back from what was probably the craziest adventure in the history of the world, well...the future of the world.

The lock on the door clicked open and startled me. I turned my head to see Rob step inside. He walked over to me cautiously. "Wren, I know you've had a really difficult time lately, but I want you to know there are people here who really care about you and want to help you." He stopped abruptly and looked down in surprise as I ran to him and squeezed him in a tight hug.

Tears of joy welled up in my eyes as I assured him, "It's over. I'm done with the time machine. I'm done with the orb." I was finished lingering in my past and trying to control everything.

As he slowly wrapped his arms around me to return my embrace, I pictured Cass as a young girl just past her teen years, with her signature black bob and tough exterior. Tolli would be younger too; maybe his blonde hair was even wilder and shaggier. Most importantly, they would all be alive. Alex wouldn't be burdened with all the stress of saving the world and he'd be...

A young man entered the room, still holding the tools he'd used to pick the lock. Dark, haphazard tufts of hair poked his eyes. I studied his face. He didn't appear worn down with grief; he looked...happy. The corners of his mouth were turned up into a gentle smile, and his silver robotics crawled up his legs and hand like always.

I grinned, trying to keep myself from running over to him. They had no clue what had happened to me and what could have happened in the future. Maybe one day I would tell them, but not today. I slipped the watch I was still holding into my pocket.

"Hi, I'm Alex Donahue." He strolled over to us.

I stepped back from Rob and looked over at Alex, returning his smile. "Wren Derecho."

"I can't believe you locked Rob out. You're pretty crazy, aren't you?" Alex whispered mischievously, glancing up at Rob standing right beside him.

I laughed loudly. "You have no idea."

As my gaze met his, I realized his eyes were a deep blue.

EPILOGUE: UNKNOWN

So, you thought I was dead?
You thought I was defeated?
You thought you got rid of me?
No, I'm not finished yet.
You believe I am only a power source, but I am so much more.
I am power.
I am control.
I am The Protector.
And my abilities are far beyond your comprehension.
I have no need for a time machine.
Time cannot contain me.
You can try to alter your fate.
But time will always correct itself.
I will stay here, floating in the abyss, waiting.
Until I am, once again, inside your head.
"Phase One: mission complete."

ACKNOWLEDGEMENTS

THANK YOU to all the people who helped make this book possible and to my family and friends who have always believed in me.

I'd like to mention these incredible people by name:

Special thanks to my mom and dad, Jeamie and Chris Nichol, who support me in everything I do. They are the best parents in the world, and I love them so much!

Thank you so much, Kirsten Marion and Common Deer Press, and to my entire publishing team who made all this possible and went out of their way to make this an extremely positive experience for me. Thanks, Bobbi Beatty, for all your hard work in editing this book. I never imagined that it could be this good! Thank you, David Moratto, for designing my official book cover. You guys are amazing!

Thank you, Cold Lake, for being a great place to live! Thanks to all the teachers I've ever had, and to every Cold Laker in my life who celebrated with me, took care of me, encouraged me, and prayed for me. There are a lot of you!

Thanks to my three siblings - Silas, Everett, and Titus — who gave me lots of feedback and suggested I change some of the characters' names. I did, and they liked those names less. Love you guys!

Thanks to my godmother and fellow writer, Grace Schienbein, who loves to take the time to talk to me about writing, who let me hang out with her on Career Day, and who always has a quiet space available for me to write.

Thanks to my grandpa, Kai Kwan, who inspired the character, Kyler Quan, and who I can always call to ask about specific details on how to break into a car (for writing purposes only). Thanks to my grandma, Eliza Kwan, for being my biggest cheerleader.

Thank you, Uncle Jamie and Auntie Renee, who were pumped about my book. My aunt was one of the first people that I sent my manuscript to and she read it as fast as she could. Wren's name is based on her nickname.

Thanks to my grandma and grandpa, Normie and Cecil Nichol, for loving me and believing in me.

Thank you, Uncle Cam and Auntie Janelle, Uncle Kevin and Auntie Cheryl, and Auntie Shuana, and all my cousins who are very excited for me!

And thanks to Earl, who inspired the character Earl.

ABOUT THE AUTHOR

Nyah Nichol was born and raised in Cold Lake, Alberta, where she currently attends high school. Her hobbies include reading, drawing, and crocheting. She has three younger siblings who can be annoying at times, but sweet and awesome the rest of the time. She has a mom and dad who love her very much and support her in everything she does.